The First Time Ever Published!

The Sixth Classic Diner Mystery

From *New York Times* Bestselling Author

Jessica Beck

A REAL PICKLE

Other Books by Jessica Beck

The Donut Shop Mysteries

Glazed Murder
Fatally Frosted
Sinister Sprinkles
Evil Éclairs
Tragic Toppings
Killer Crullers
Drop Dead Chocolate
Powdered Peril
Illegally Iced
Deadly Donuts

The Classic Diner Mysteries

A Chili Death
A Deadly Beef
A Killer Cake
A Baked Ham
A Bad Egg
A Real Pickle

The Ghost Cat Cozy Mysteries

Ghost Cat: Midnight Paws
Ghost Cat 2: Bid for Midnight

Jessica Beck is the *New York Times* Bestselling Author of the Donut Shop Mysteries, the Classic Diner Mystery Series, and the Ghost Cat Cozy Mysteries.

To my daughter, Emily

Chapter 1

If you had asked me *before* it happened, I would have said that it was impossible to murder a dead man, but that's exactly what happened inside The Charming Moose late one afternoon in October. There was really no other way to look at it; we were in a real pickle when Curtis Trane dropped dead in our diner after taking a bite of one of the pancakes my mother was so famous for. Usually Jasper Fork, North Carolina, wasn't known for its high homicide rate, so naturally my thoughts didn't immediately go to murder when I saw Curtis slumped over in his booth. The pickle fortune heir was dying and had been for several months; that much everyone who saw him knew. His chauffeur, butler, and best friend, Jeffrey, had told us the first time we'd met Curtis that he wasn't long for this world, and his employer was determined to get every last bit of life out of it that he could. Spending his fortune as his life wasted away was one of the last joys left him, and he was taking full advantage of it. The small toy pickles he left everywhere were a testament to his family's wealth, but his smiles despite the pain said more about who the man himself was.

And now he was gone.

I hurried toward the booth when I first spotted Curtis slumped over. A minute before, a stranger had stumbled into his booth, said his excuses, and then left the diner. I didn't give it another thought, and it wasn't until I looked back at Curtis that I saw that he was in obvious trouble. There were a handful of folks in the diner, and I was thrilled to see Laney Jones enjoying some bacon and eggs before she started her shift as a pediatrics nurse. "Laney, help me," I said urgently.

Her smile faded when she saw Curtis. That woman couldn't have weighed more than ninety pounds soaking wet, but she looked as though she could run through walls as she sped to my friend's side in her Snoopy scrubs. As she checked for a pulse, I turned to everyone else at the diner. They were all starting to stand up and move toward Curtis's table, but I couldn't let them get in her way. "Please, would everyone stay where you are and give Laney some room to work?"

There were a few nods from my customers, and everyone did as I asked as they sat back in their chairs. My mother came out of the kitchen to see what was going on, and Ellen Hightower, our breakfast and lunch server, pulled her off to one side and quickly caught her up to date. I was glad that she did, because I had my hands full at the moment. I looked around at my seated customers and realized that their breakfast meals were all but forgotten as they watched Laney work on Curtis.

"Somebody needs to call 911," Laney told me after she'd gently pulled him to the floor and was administering CPR. "I'm going to need some help here."

"I've got it," Reverend Mercer said. The pastor's wife was out of town yet again, which explained his presence in our diner that morning. Miriam, his wife, didn't allow him to eat at The Charming Moose, but that never kept the good reverend from visiting us whenever she was gone.

As Laney worked, I asked her, "How's he doing?"

She didn't say a word as she continued her efforts to revive him, but she did glance at me for a split second, and from the expression on her face, I knew that it wasn't good.

An ambulance drove up with lights flashing and siren wailing, and as they rushed into the diner, I saw Jeffrey close on their heels. I had to stop him before he got to his boss.

"What happened?" the chauffeur asked as I tried to restrain him. "Let me go, Victoria. Can't you see that he needs me?"

I didn't move, though. "Jeffrey, what he needs right now, he's getting. You have to let them work if they're going to have any chance at all of helping him."

"This is all too soon," Jeffrey said as he slumped against me. Tears were tracking down his cheeks as he spoke. "I thought he had at least another good month left in him."

"We never know when these things are going to happen," I said, doing my best to ease his anguish.

"Somehow *he* knew," Jeffrey said.

The emergency rescue crew loaded Curtis gently onto the stretcher and started to wheel him out of the diner.

"I'm going with you," Jeffrey demanded.

"Are you family?" one of the EMTs asked him.

"I'm the closest person in the world to him," Jeffrey said. "That should count for something."

The EMT looked at me with a question in his glance, and I nodded. If Curtis managed to come back from this, I knew that there was no one that he'd rather see than Jeffrey. I was certain that their relationship had started off as employer and employee, but Curtis had admitted to me once that Jeffrey was the closest thing he had ever had to a real son.

"Let's go," Laney said, and Jeffrey was right on her heels.

As the ambulance pulled away, I was surprised to see Sheriff Croft drive up and park hurriedly in front of the café.

"What's going on, Sheriff?" I asked.

"I need to secure the scene before anyone touches anything, Victoria," he said officiously.

The very idea that it might not have been natural causes shocked me to my core. "You can't be serious, Sheriff. The man was dying."

"It's my job to make sure that no one tried to help him along," he said. As Karen Morgan, our Clerk of Court, got up to pay her bill, the sheriff added, "If everyone will please stay where they are seated, I'll get around to you in a few minutes."

Karen clearly wasn't very happy about that. "Edgar Croft, I have an important department to run at city hall."

"I know that, Karen, but you're going to have to do things my way right now."

She frowned, but I was glad to see that she took her seat

again. The faster the sheriff could do what he had to do, the sooner I'd be able to send my customers on their way. A sudden thought occurred to me. Why would that be a *good* thing for me? There were a dozen diners in The Charming Moose at the moment, but once they were free to go wherever they wanted to, the stories of Curtis's demise would spread through the town like a firestorm, and I would have to find a way to defend my diner's reputation yet again. When I'd taken the place over after my dad's brief time at the helm, I never dreamed the type of problems I'd find myself in the middle of. Had my grandfather, Moose, had to deal with these kinds of situations when he'd run the place for all those years? Somehow I doubted it.

One of the sheriff's deputies came in with a video camera, and a digital camera as well. "Get all the shots you need," Sheriff Croft said as he stepped away.

It was a good time to corner the sheriff. "Is all of this really necessary?"

"Victoria, a man died here this morning," Croft said as he watched his deputy work.

"Don't you think I know that?" I said in an aggravated whisper. "He was more than just a customer, Sheriff. Curtis Trane was my friend."

The sheriff finally looked at me, and he nodded sadly as he said, "I'm sorry for your loss, but I have to follow strict procedure here."

"He had cancer," I explained. "According to his chauffeur, he should have been dead a year ago."

"I understand all of that, but I still have to finish up here. I'll make it as quick and as painless as I can, but the work needs to be done."

I knew better than to buck the sheriff while he was performing his official duties, so I saved my breath. "Is there anything that I can do to help?" I asked.

"You can stand outside and turn away anybody who wants to come in," he said.

"How's that going to look?" I asked.

"Not good, but it's going to be better than if one of my people does it," he said tersely.

The man had a point at that.

I walked outside, hoping beyond hope that nobody would want breakfast for the next half hour, but of course, that didn't happen.

As I started to tell the eighth customer why he they couldn't come in, I saw a familiar pickup truck drive up. It stopped quickly in front of the diner, and my grandfather got out, looking mad enough to spit nails. Great. This was just one more complication that I didn't need on what had started out to be a perfectly lovely morning in October.

There was no chance of me salvaging the day now. I'd miss Curtis terribly even though I'd known since we'd first met that he was going to die soon, but I couldn't let myself dwell on the loss at the moment. I had to deal with my grandfather and then the sheriff. Later I'd find time to mourn for my friend appropriately, but for now, I'd have to do my best to save the business that my grandfather had started and that I hoped to carry on.

"What happened?" Moose asked as he peered into the diner. "And more importantly, what are you doing out here instead of in there?" The last comment was flavored with a gesture toward the diner. That was Moose, never afraid of making his point with his hands.

"Curtis Trane died in one of our booths," I said, wondering how many times I'd have to say that in the next few hours, even days.

"Then you should be in there," Moose said, his voice a little calmer now.

"The sheriff has closed us down for now, Moose. He thought it might be easier for our customers to hear it from me instead of one of his people, and I agreed with him wholeheartedly."

"Why is he closing us down? It was natural causes, wasn't it?"

"I don't see how it could have been anything else, but the sheriff has his heart set on doing his job."

"We'll just see about that," my grandfather said heatedly as he started to walk past me.

I put a hand on his chest. "Hold your horses."

"Victoria, I need to be in there right now."

"Moose, what you really need to do is to take a deep breath and let it out slowly. We both know that if you go in there blustering like a madman, you're just going to make things worse."

He feigned surprise by my description. "I'll have you know that I've never blustered in my life, young lady."

I tried not to laugh, honestly I did, but the grimness in the air must have done something to me. At first I cracked a small smile, but soon enough, it was a full-blown grin. "Seriously? Are you going to really try to convince me of that? I've known you my entire life, you know."

"I don't bluster," he repeated, but then his voice softened as he added, "Maybe I raise my voice on occasion, but it's just to be heard."

It was still a downright lie, but I decided to let it slide. "If we stay out of his way, it will be over soon enough and life can get back to normal for us."

"Face it, Victoria, life has never been all that normal for us, even on our best days."

"I'll grant you that," I said as I peeked inside. The photographer had wrapped up, and the sheriff was moving quickly from table to table, taking the names down of our customers. "Maybe we should go inside now after all."

"I'm one step ahead of you," Moose said as he hurried past me. The sheriff finished taking down every name, and as he closed his notebook, he announced, "I have one question for each of you, and then you're all free to go. Did anyone see anything unusual at the diner this morning?"

Most folks shook their heads, but Francie Humphries, the woman who owned the only bakery in town, spoke up. "Do you mean *besides* the man who tripped on a chair and nearly landed in that poor man's lap a minute before he died?"

"I saw that, too," I said. "Did you get a good look at his face, Francie? I couldn't see it behind that hooded sweatshirt he was wearing."

"I'll ask the questions here, if you don't mind," the sheriff told me, and then he turned to Francie. "Can you describe him?"

"I was in the same position that Victoria was in; I only saw him from behind, and I didn't give him more than a moment's thought. I couldn't even guess about how old he was or what he looked like. Like I said, it all happened so fast that I barely knew what was happening."

"Did anyone else see this incident?" the sheriff asked.

The Reverend Mercer said haltingly, "I don't mean to contradict you, Francie, but I saw it, too, and I was certain that it was a woman."

"It was a man, Father," she said, and then she added a little uncertainly, "At least I think it was a man. Maybe. I'm not sure."

I shook my head as I realized that I hadn't been able to tell, either. So, either a man or a woman had stumbled into Curtis's booth just before he'd died. Since I doubted that it had scared him and given him a heart attack, I wasn't at all sure what good the information would do the sheriff, at any rate.

Sheriff Croft nodded, jotted a few lines into his book, and then he asked, "Is there anything else anyone wants to add?"

When no one else spoke up, the sheriff closed his notebook once more. "Okay. You're all free to go. Thank you for your cooperation."

Now it was my diners' turn to ask questions. "Who was that man in the booth?"

"Was he really murdered?" someone else asked.

"I thought he looked kind of sickly when he walked in," another diner said.

"Folks, I don't have any answers for you right now. I'm just collecting information."

That seemed to satisfy no one, and as the sheriff started to leave, I asked, “Can we resume business now, Sheriff Croft?”

“I don’t see why not,” he said. “I’ve got samples of his food and drink, and I’ve had the scene thoroughly photographed and filmed. I’m not sure that I’d use that booth until you can give it a proper scrubbing, but other than that, carry on.”

“Thanks,” I said. I decided that we’d clean it indeed, but not with everyone watching us. I blocked the booth with a pair of chairs, and then I turned to our customers. “Folks, listen up. I’m sorry about what happened and that you had to be here to witness it. Your meals this morning are on the house, but we’re going to have to close the place for an hour now so we can get things ready for lunch. I hope you all have a great day, and come back to The Charming Moose again soon. Thanks again.”

As they filed out, each and every one of them glancing toward the booth where Curtis had died, I did my best to smile at them all, despite the sadness in my heart. After the front door was locked tight and the OPEN sign flipped to CLOSED, I turned to Moose. “I’m willing to bet that you think I was too extravagant just now giving everyone a free meal, don’t you?”

“On the contrary, it was exactly the right thing to do,” Moose said. “I heartily approve. It won’t keep folks from talking about the diner and what happened here, but it might give us a little positive publicity, which couldn’t be a bad thing right now.”

Mom came out of the kitchen with a bucket, a scrub brush, and a rag.

“I’ll take that, Mom,” I said as I reached for her little cleaning kit.

“Nonsense. I don’t mind doing it,” she said.

“I know, but I’m sure that you’ve got your hands full in the kitchen right now,” I insisted. I didn’t want my mother to have to deal with that booth, not while I was ready and able to handle it myself.

"I'll do it," Moose said. "This place was mine from the start. That makes it my responsibility."

I thought about fighting him over it since *I* was the one who ran The Charming Moose now, but did I really want to win that particular argument? "Thanks," I said. "You win."

He raised one eyebrow as he looked at me. "Victoria, you gave up surprisingly easy just then."

"What can I say?" I asked with a grin. "Growing up, I was always taught to respect my elders."

He just laughed, and I was happy to see my mother willingly giving up the cleaning supplies to her father-in-law.

"Ellen," my mother said, "if you bus the tables, I'll get things started in back. We should easily be ready to reopen in under an hour." Mom looked back at me as she added, "If that's still the plan."

"I don't see why not," I said. "What do you think, Moose?"

"The quicker we're open again, the less time rumors have to spread that we killed somebody here today," he said matter-of-factly.

"Do you honestly think that anyone's going to say that?" I asked him.

"You're naïve if you think for one second that they're not," he said. "Don't worry, Victoria. This too shall pass."

"I hope you're right," I said, but I suspected that my grandfather was wrong.

I just didn't know *how* wrong at the time.

Chapter 2

"He didn't make it," Jeffrey said solemnly as he walked back into The Charming Moose two hours later. He looked as though he'd just lost his best friend, and I didn't doubt that it was true. I knew from past experience that the two of them had been very close.

"I'm so sorry for your loss," I said as I touched his shoulder lightly.

"Thanks. I appreciate that," he said. "You know, Curtis hired me away from his sister, Charlotte, and brought me here three years ago. I've been an orphan most of my life, and that man ended up being the only family that I ever really had."

"How did that all come about?" I asked. Clearly the man needed to talk to someone, and I would have to do.

"Charlotte hired me out of high school to drive for her in San Francisco," he said. "The odd thing was, she was only at the house for a month or two each year. The rest of time, the staff just tried to entertain ourselves waiting for her to come back. Three years ago though, her brother showed up unexpectedly, and Curtis and I hit it off from the start. He asked me to come work for him back here on a full-time basis, and I jumped at the chance." Jeffrey let out a deep sigh, and then he added, "That was a long time ago, though. I still can't believe that he's gone."

"What are you going to do with yourself now?" I asked him.

"I'm not quite sure, but I know one thing: I'm not going back to work for Charlotte."

"Was she that bad as an employer?"

"I don't know if I can say that, but once I worked for Curtis, I knew that she and I were finished. I suppose I'll find something, but I saved my money, so I don't have to do anything drastic right away." He looked back at the limo, and then Jeffrey added, "After I take that back to the house, I suppose my work is done. You don't happen to know of any places around here for rent, do you? I don't need much, just a one bedroom apartment."

"Let me call a real estate agent I know," I said. "If you can wait, I'll see if she's free right now."

"Don't go to any trouble on my account," Jeffrey said.

"It's no trouble at all. She's a customer here." I dialed Diane Meadows's number.

She picked up on the first ring. "Meadows Properties," she said automatically.

"Diane, it's Victoria Nelson. I need a favor. Do you have any one-bedroom apartments available?"

"Oh, no. I can't believe this," she said. Diane was clearly upset about something.

"What's wrong?" I asked her.

"You and Greg are splitting up. Victoria, how can you be so calm about it?"

"What? No. We're not. Where did you even get that idea?"

"You just asked me for a one-bedroom apartment, Victoria. It doesn't take a leap in logic to know what that means."

"You need to get that imagination of yours in check," I said with a laugh. "Greg and I are fine. It's for a friend of mine, a man named Jeffrey…" I held the phone to my shoulder as I asked the chauffeur, "What's your last name?"

"Graham," he said.

I put the phone off my shoulder. "Jeffrey Graham. I'll vouch for him personally, Diane. He's a good guy."

"I've got two places at the moment, depending on how much he has to spend. If he's loaded, I've got a real beauty that just came on the market."

"That sounds good, but let's go in the other direction," I said. I didn't want to come right out and say that Jeffrey wasn't rich, but then again, I didn't want Diane trying to set him up with something well beyond his budget.

"Got it," she said. "If he doesn't mind Spartan surroundings, I've got a real deal for him."

"Let me check," I said, and then I asked Jeffrey, "How do you feel about a simple place?"

He grinned broadly. "I love it."

"He'd like to see it," I told Diane.

"Have him come by my office at three this afternoon, and I'll show it to him. Thanks for the lead, Victoria."

"Thank you," I said.

As I jotted Diane's address and phone number down on a napkin, I told Jeffrey, "I assume that you'll be free by three this afternoon."

"I'll be there," he said as he took the note from me. "Wow, I thought stories about small towns were all lies."

"What do you mean?"

"You hardly know me, and yet look at all that you've done for me already."

I smiled. "I like the way you looked after your boss," I said. "That makes you a good guy in my book. Don't let me down, okay? I vouched for you, after all."

"I wouldn't dream of it," he said. "Well, I'd better get moving if I'm going to get everything done in time for my meeting with Ms. Meadows."

"If you need a different appointment time, I can always call her back."

"No, I should be fine. There's really not all that much left for me to do. Thanks again."

"You're most welcome," I said. "Jeffrey, would you do me a favor?"

"Anything," he said.

"Be careful what you promise," I said with a smile. "This shouldn't be too difficult, though. Will you drop by and tell me when the funeral's scheduled? I'd like to go."

"I'm sorry, but I can't."

I was a little hurt by his outright refusal. "Why, is it for family only?"

"That's not it. You see, there isn't going to be one. Curtis didn't believe in them. He *never* focused on his death while he was alive, and he didn't want us to after he left us. He'll be cremated within the hour, and his ashes will be spread under his favorite oak tree on his property. It's the way that he wanted it—no fuss and no muss."

"I can understand that," I said. "I'll miss him and the tiny plastic pickles he used to leave behind."

"If you'd like some, I have three boxes of them in the limo," Jeffrey said. "He never wanted to run out. I guess in the end, he didn't."

A tear started tracking down his cheek, and Jeffrey left the diner quickly before he lost it completely.

Ellen came over and joined me after he was gone. "It's so sad, isn't it?"

"I'm surprised by how hard it hit me. It's not like it was a big secret that Curtis was dying, but I hate that it happened here at the diner."

"Me, too," she said as she looked over at the booth where he'd died. "Am I crazy, or is there a white shadow hanging over that booth?"

I looked where she was pointing, and sure enough, it appeared that a ghostly image was hovering above the surface of the table. Feeling a little shaky, I started walking toward it, determined to see what was causing it. My hand went right through it, and I looked down at the napkin dispenser. The stainless steel surface was reflecting sunlight off the tabletop and into the air. I moved it a quarter turn, and the spectral image suddenly disappeared.

"It's gone!" Ellen said loudly.

"Take it easy. It was just a reflection."

She shivered noticeably. "It still gives me the creeps. I'm glad that my shift's about over. Thanks for letting me take off an hour early today." Ellen usually worked until two, but she'd asked for permission to duck out early today, and I hadn't seen any reason not to accommodate her.

"You can take off now, if you'd like."

"No, I'll wait it out," Ellen replied.

Wayne, the mechanic who was sweet on her, came by the diner ten minutes later to pick her up. Ellen still had five minutes left on her abbreviated shift, but I told her, "Go on. I'll see you tomorrow."

"Bye," she said as she put her arm through Wayne's. They had gone through some tough times lately, but it was finally starting to look like they just might make it.

Greg came out of the kitchen as they left and smiled at me. "It's just the two of us now," he said. "Care for a quick bite to eat before things get crazy again? I know for a fact that your lunch was interrupted twice by customers, and you ended up throwing most of it away, so you've got to be starving."

"I could eat," I said, answering his smile with one of my own. "What did you have in mind?"

"Would grilled cheese sandwiches and chicken soup be too plain for you?"

"Not if you're the one who makes them," I said. Greg had a knack for taking the most mundane ingredients and turning them into the most delightful meals.

"Two of each, coming right up."

As he ducked back to the grill to make our food, I looked around the diner. There were fewer customers than I'd hoped for at that time of day, but it might not have been because of what had happened at the diner earlier. It could just be part of the lull we usually experienced between the lunch and dinner crowds. I just hoped they found their way back to us, and quickly. We couldn't afford to have too many customers leaving us, not if we were going to keep The Charming Moose afloat.

"I'm afraid that I have some bad news," Sheriff Croft said when he walked into the diner a little later.

"Thanks, but we already heard," I said.

He looked shocked by my admission. "How is that possible? I know that Jasper Fork is a small town, but somebody's going to jail for this."

"Take it easy," I said. "Jeffrey came by earlier to let us know that Curtis didn't make it. There's no reason to lock him up for it."

"Is that *all* that you know?" he asked me.

"What else could there be?" What was the sheriff talking about?

"It was murder, Victoria," he said softly.

"Murder?" I asked, no doubt much louder than he would have wanted. I couldn't help myself. Someone had killed a friend of mine in my diner! "Was it poison?" I asked softly. That was every restaurateur's nightmare, and I was no exception. We could lose our business if someone had slipped something into Curtis's meal.

"No, he was stabbed in the chest with a thin metal rod, and it went straight into his heart. The poor man didn't stand a chance. Whoever did it left the weapon in, so there wasn't very much blood at all, and with the red shirt he was wearing, it was easy to miss. The EMTs found it on the way to the hospital, but I ordered them to keep a lid on what they found until I had time to investigate. That's why I was threatening to lock somebody up for telling *you* about it."

"Jeffrey just assumed that it was cancer that killed his boss," I said. "Sheriff Croft, why would someone murder a man so close to death anyway?"

"That's what I aim to find out," he said. "It's probably crazy for me to even ask you this, but you're not going to stay out of this case, are you?"

I shook my head. "You know that I can't. He was my friend, and someone killed him in The Charming Moose. What choice do I have?"

"You could be patient and let me do my job," he said a little impatiently.

"Be reasonable. Moose and I might be able to go places you can't," I said. "You should trust me enough by now to know that if we find something significant, we'll come to you with it."

"I do, and I appreciate it, but this killer is something I haven't seen before. Killing Curtis Trane in front of a room full of people sounds sociopathic to me." He shook his head as he added, "I don't know anybody who could get into the head of a killer like that."

"I'm not afraid," I said, though that wasn't strictly true.

The sheriff looked at me skeptically. "If you're not lying, then I'm even more concerned about you. Victoria, you should be terrified."

"Well, maybe a little," I said. "Are you afraid?"

"Let's just put it this way. I'm glad that I'm armed all of the time. I can't tell you how strongly I recommend that you sit this one out. Leave the investigation to people who have been trained and are paid to take the risks."

Greg popped out of the kitchen, noticed me talking to the sheriff, and raised his eyebrows. I blinked slowly, and he stepped back into the kitchen. We were so in synch that we could communicate volumes with glances, and I knew that I'd be lost without him. There was no doubt in my mind that he would be devastated as well if something happened to me. Did I have the right to risk my life? When I'd taken my vows with Greg, I'd made a promise to him forever after. Was I breaking it now?

"Victoria, what are you going to do?" the sheriff asked me.

"I can't make any promises one way or the other," I said. I couldn't, either, at least not to him.

"I figured as much," he said. "Just be careful, okay? And tell that crazy old grandfather of yours the same thing."

"That I can do," I said. "Thanks for letting me know."

"It will be out soon enough. I'm not naïve enough to think that I can delay the news much longer. Folks are going to react to this; you know that, don't you? Some will come by to see where it happened, but you won't be able to get others within ten miles of this place. You should expect rumors of poison to start surfacing, too. After all, *we* know that he was stabbed, but most folks won't let the facts keep them from telling a good story, and being poisoned to death in a diner is going to be too good to pass up, no matter what the truth might be."

"We'll deal with that when we come to it," I said. "Just catch whoever did this."

"I'll do my best," he said.

Moose came in half an hour later. "So, how are we going to tackle this?" he asked me with a grim expression on his face.

"Tackle what?"

"Haven't you heard the news? It's already all over town. Somebody stabbed Curtis Trane in our diner right under our noses. We're not going to let them get away with it, are we?"

"I'm not so sure we should dig into this one," I said hesitantly.

"What? Why not?" He looked hard at me for a few seconds, and then my grandfather asked me, "Victoria, are you spooked by this case?"

"Aren't you?" I asked him. "The sheriff came by to tell me what happened, and he put some pretty dark thoughts into my head while he was here."

"What did he say? Did he scare you?" Moose asked.

"Let's just say that he pointed a few things out to me that I should have seen myself. Moose, the cases we've worked on in the past have been pretty tame compared to this."

"Nonsense. We've tracked down killers before," Moose said.

"Yes, but they haven't been psychopaths, either."

"What makes you think this murderer is any different?"

"The killer acted boldly in a crowded diner," I said. "Doesn't that strike you as someone who doesn't care if they're caught or not?"

"I think it was probably pretty savvy, actually."

"What do you mean?"

"When is the *only* time that you've ever seen Curtis

without Jeffrey close behind him?" Moose asked me. "I know for a fact that the only time it happened when I noticed was when Curtis was here having a meal."

"Why would the killer strike in front of a dozen people instead of in plain sight of just one? It doesn't make sense."

"Not if Jeffrey is everything that he appears to be, but what if he's not?"

"What else could he be?" I asked.

"I'm not sure, but it's something that I'd like to ask him."

"I still don't understand," I said.

"That's because my cynical old mind is working overtime on this. I've got a hunch that Jeffrey is more than he's shown us so far."

"You honestly don't think that he's a bad guy, do you?" The thought appalled me. It went against the Jeffrey that I knew, but that didn't mean that I might not be wrong. I was a decent judge of character, but sometimes I ran into someone who could fool me just as much as he did everyone else.

"I'm not saying that. All I'm saying is what if he was Curtis's bodyguard as well as being his driver?"

"I suppose that it's possible," I said.

"If I'm right, which would you rather face? A dozen uninterested strangers, or one very determined man trained to protect his charge?"

"You could be right," I said.

Moose looked up, clearly surprised by what he saw. "Well, speak of the devil and he appears."

"What are you talking about now?"

"Look," he said as he pointed over my shoulder.

Jeffrey was headed toward the diner with a determined expression on his face. It would give us the perfect opportunity to question him about his resume, but I wasn't sure what purpose it would serve at this point.

After all, Curtis Trane was dead, and no new information we might get about his chauffeur would bring him back.

"Let's see what he wants before we start grilling him," I

said to Moose as Jeffrey came in the door.

"I need to speak with you," the chauffeur said as he approached us.

"This isn't about the apartment, is it?" I asked, knowing in my heart that whatever Jeffrey wanted to discuss was a great deal more dire than his current housing situation.

"No, I'm staying right where I am, at least for now. I already called Ms. Meadows and canceled our appointment."

"That's good news then, isn't it?" I asked.

"It doesn't matter to me where I stay one way or the other, to be honest with you," Jeffrey said.

"Can Moose hang around for this conversation, too?" I asked. "I don't have any secrets from my grandfather, or any of my family, for that matter."

"As a matter of fact, I need him to stay. He's a part of this, too," Jeffrey said as he waved an envelope in the air. "Is there somewhere more private that we can talk?"

"Why not over there?" I asked as I pointed to a booth in the corner. The diner had only a few customers at the moment, but that didn't mean that I could just leave my post.

"It should do just fine," he said.

As we walked to the booth, my grandfather asked casually, "Jeffrey, were you ever a cop, or maybe in the military, before you became a chauffeur?"

Jeffrey stopped and looked carefully at my grandfather before he spoke. "What makes you ask me that?"

"I know it was one or the other," Moose said with much more confidence in his guess than I would have ever been able to muster.

"Neither one, actually," Jeffrey said with a slight grin. "But I've been taking karate and other self-defense classes nearly all my life, so I know how to handle myself in just about any situation."

"So then, you were more than just a chauffeur."

Jeffrey shrugged. "Let's just say that Curtis was pleased with my particular skill-set. Does that answer your question?"

"It does," Moose said.

"Now, what do you need from us?" I asked the chauffeur once we were all seated.

"It's not for me," Jeffrey said. "I've got something for you both from Curtis."

I was shocked by the news. "Did he actually leave us something in his will?"

"I'm afraid it's nothing as straightforward as that," Jeffrey said. "To my surprise, it turns out that I'm his executor, so if you do inherit something from him, that will all come later. This was in a bigger envelope marked URGENT, OPEN IN CASE OF MY DEATH, and I have to admit that I've been curious about it since it came into my hands. I found the packet last week in my room, and I asked him about it. All Curtis would tell me was that when the time was right, I'd know what to do with the letters inside, so that's why I'm here."

"Would you mind explaining what you mean by that?" I asked.

"There's no need. Curtis did that himself. You both need to read this. Take your time. I'm not going anywhere."

Chapter 3

Jeffrey opened the envelope and pulled out two single sheets of paper. I thought it might be something long, but it was actually two copies of the same document. Moose got one, and I got the other one.

To Moose and Victoria,

We haven't known each other very long, but what is time when we weigh friendships? We three have common spirits, a thirst for knowledge and a desire to see things made right. I need you both to do something for me, and I beg you to take me up on my offer.

You see, if you're reading this, I've been murdered. What a surprising turn of events! I expected cancer to rob me of my life, but it appears that someone has been a tad impatient waiting on the disease that has stolen so much from me already.

I know why I've been murdered, or at least I suspect I know. You see, I'm in the process of changing my will, and it appears that one of my heirs didn't like the changes I was about to implement. You might think it simple for me to make the changes I sought, but I'm afraid that it's much more complicated than that on the scale of my amassed wealth.

There are several people who would benefit from me dying early, I'm sad to say. These include: my sister, Charlotte Trane; my niece, Sarah Harper; and my nephew, Tristan Wellborne. Chris Crane, my business manager, must also be a candidate, as he's been acting suspiciously around me lately. I can't prove anything, though, so I'm hesitant to act just yet.

I realize that it's not much to go on, but it's all that I've got for you.

I hate funerals. I always have, and the prospect of having something morbid held for my sake repels me beyond explanation, but I'm afraid that it's the only avenue I have to offer you both further assistance. I'm sure that Jeffrey will be shocked to learn of my plans for a memorial service, but once he reads this, I hope that he understands the necessity of it.

Victoria and Moose, I know of your past successes in solving murder, and I need you to solve mine. It is a dying request, one that I hope you won't refuse.

You are cordially invited to my home for the next three days and two nights in Laurel Landing to bring my killer to justice. Rooms have been set aside for you, and I ask that you leave immediately and return to my home with Jeffrey. He'll stop long enough for each of you to pack a bag, but then I ask that you stay until you find my killer, or until the final service is held, whichever comes first.

I understand this will put your diner under some hardship, so I've instructed my bank to transfer more than sufficient funds into your account to make up for any potential income you're about to lose.

Of course you can choose to ignore my last request, keep the money or give it back, but I have high hopes that you'll respect my last wishes.

I wish you good luck, and happy hunting!

Your friend,

Curtis

I read it twice before I spoke. Moose was patiently waiting for me to finish it again. Jeffrey just sat there, not giving anything away.

"Is this on the level?" I asked.

"I've received my instructions," he said. "You should also know that I'm staying on at the house now at least until after the services, so I'll be in my little apartment over the garage. *Your* accommodations will be a bit nicer." He said the last part with the ghost of a smile, and I wondered if it was some kind of private joke that he'd shared with his late employer and friend. "So, what do you think? I know that it's asking a lot of you, but I hope you'll do it. Curtis was quite impressed when he learned that you had both solved murder cases before."

"How did he hear about them?" I asked him.

"Victoria, I shouldn't have to tell you that this is a small town, and my employer liked talking to people. More than one resident of Jasper Fork regaled him with stories of your past victories over crime."

"We've had a few successes," Moose acknowledged, "but that doesn't mean that we'll necessarily be able to figure out what happened to him. I wasn't even *at* the diner when he was murdered."

"I *was* there, but I might as well have been someplace else," I said. "I still can't believe that someone killed him right in front of a room full of diners, including me."

"Will you do it, then?"

"I have a question," I asked. "The letter mentioned payment for closing the diner. Is that a *requirement* for our help?"

"What do you mean?" Jeffrey asked.

"She's wondering if we can still keep the place open even if we go," Moose said, and then he looked at me. "That's what you want to know, right?"

"I just keep thinking that if we get Martha to cover for me most of the time and ask the girls to extend their normal shifts, they should all be able to function just fine without me for three days."

"You're not as easy to replace as you might think," Moose said, "but you make a valid point. We could even get Stephanie in to run the register so Martha doesn't feel the full weight of replacing you on her shoulders."

Stephanie Black had worked for my grandfather for a while when he'd been running The Charming Moose, but that had been several years ago. "Do you think she'd do it? I know that she quit quite suddenly."

"She eloped with Nathan Black and hung me out to dry," Moose said with a smile. "But Nathan's gone, and I know for a fact that Stephanie is looking for some part-time work."

"She didn't approach you for a job at the diner, did she?" I asked.

Moose held both hands up, as if he were trying to defend himself. "It's nothing like that, Victoria. She knows who's running the place now."

"Good," I said. I wasn't too keen about having any of Moose's former employees going to him for a job at *my* diner. I knew that it was still the family business, but *I* was the head of it now.

"Should I call her for you?" Moose asked.

"Not so fast." I turned to Jeffrey. "How long do we have to decide?"

He shrugged. "You should take your time. I'm thinking five minutes, how about you?"

"Could we have an hour?" I asked.

"In all seriousness, if we're at the house in forty-five minutes, we should be fine. It takes thirty to get there, but I can make it in twenty. That gives you twenty-five minutes to decide and pack enough clothes to hold you."

"We can do that," I said. "Moose, call Martha and tell her that we need her here, and then call my mother and tell her the same thing."

"What are you going to do while I'm doing that?" he asked me.

"I'm going to run our last three customers out, lock the doors, and then I'm going to have a long chat with my husband."

"What about Stephanie?" Moose asked me.

I shook my head. "If we don't all agree on this, there won't even *be* any need to call her," I said. "You'd better scoot."

He grabbed his cellphone as I told Jeffrey, "You're welcome to stay, but things are going to be crazy around here for the next little while."

The chauffeur glanced at his watch. "There's something I need to do myself. I'll be back in fifteen minutes."

"Jeffrey, I'll need a little more time than that," I said.
"Then I'll wait in the car. Victoria, I hope you do this. It was important to Curtis, so that makes it important to me."
"We'll talk again soon," I said as I showed him out. I had a hunch that he wouldn't be able to keep Moose and me away from that house with a court order, but I'd meant what I'd said. We *all* had to agree, or we weren't going to do it.

"Greg, we need to talk," I said as I walked back into the kitchen.
He tensed up immediately. "That is never something a man wants to hear from the woman he loves, Victoria. Whatever I did, I can fix it. Just give me another chance."
"There's nothing wrong, you big goof," I said as I kissed his cheek.
"Good. What's up?"
"I'm going away for three days," I said.
"Okay, *now* I'm worried *again*," he said. "Unless I'm coming with you."
"Sorry, but Moose and I were the only ones who were invited." I brought him up to date about Curtis's letter.
He began nodding immediately. "Of course! You need to do this, but there's no reason to shut the place down. We can make it without you for three days, as hard as it might be." He'd added the last bit when he'd seen my frown start to form. Nobody liked to hear that they could easily be replaced, and I was no exception, especially since I was supposed to be the one in charge. "It might take its toll on Martha, though. Is there anybody else we can get in on a temporary basis?"
"Moose suggested we call Stephanie Black," I said.
"She'll do," he said.
"But not as good as I would, right?"
"Right. Victoria, do you feel safe staying out there with a killer?"
"I hadn't really thought about it," I admitted. "Moose will be with me. I'm sure that we'll both be fine."

"Just watch your step, and keep your eyes open."

"I plan to," I said as I kissed him again. "Thanks for worrying about me."

"Hey, don't thank me. It's what I do," he said.

Moose came into the back with a grin. "Martha's on her way, but I told her about the offer, and she's all for it. Your mother is in favor of it, too, by the way. If Greg agrees, then it's unanimous."

"It is," I said. "Go ahead and call Stephanie."

"That's not going to happen," Moose said.

"Why not?"

He handed me a phone number. "*You're* the one in charge. If you want her, you call her."

I felt a little bad about my earlier snit. "I don't mind, Moose. It's okay."

"You might as well take the number, Victoria. Where do you think you got that stubborn streak you're so proud of?" Moose asked me.

"I'm not stubborn," I said, and I watched as both men fought the grins that were struggling to free themselves. "I like to think of myself as a woman who knows her own mind."

"You do that, all right," Moose said.

Greg grinned broadly as he nodded. "I couldn't have put it better myself."

I smiled at both of them. "It's a good thing that I love both of you lunks as much as I do. Call her, Moose; you know her a lot better than I do. Just remind her that you're calling on my behalf."

"I can do that. What kind of hours would you like her to work?"

I thought about my current schedule, and then I told him, "If she can come in from six a.m. until two, then Martha can work two until we close."

"I'll do it," Moose said. He glanced at his watch, and then my grandfather said, "I hate to rush you, but we've got eleven minutes until we have to start packing."

"They'll be here in time," I said. Though my mother and grandmother had both given their approval to the plan, I still wanted to hear it from them in person. I was asking a favor from them, so I wanted to do it face to face.

They agreed in person when they got to the diner, and Stephanie jumped at the chance to come back to The Charming Moose, even if it was based on just three days' work. If she did okay, I might put her on part-time. Greg and I had been dying to get away for quite some time, and if I could trust Stephanie and Martha to work the front and put Moose on the grill instead of Greg, we might actually have a chance to experience a real vacation. The money Curtis was depositing couldn't go for anything better, as far as I was concerned.

There was a tap at the front door, and I opened it for Jeffrey. "What's your decision?" he asked.

"We'll do it," I said. "Moose, are you coming?" I called out.

"Try to go without me," my grandfather said as he came bustling out of the kitchen.

The relief on Jeffrey's face was clear. "I'm so glad that you both decided to help."

"We didn't know Curtis as well or for as long as you did, but he was our friend, too," I said.

"He felt the same way about the two of you."

It felt odd riding in the back of a limousine to my house, but I might be able to learn to live with such luxury. "What should we bring with us?" I asked as I looked down at my blue jeans and old T-shirt.

"They've all been warned that you are both eccentric in your clothing choices," Jeffrey said. "You'll need something black for the service, but the rest of time, wear whatever you'd like to. Curtis liked to dress casually, so no one will be surprised by your informal style."

I took his advice and packed a quick bag, but Moose was even faster when we got to his place. While Jeffrey and I were waiting in the limo, I asked him, "What do you think about that letter we got? I'm assuming that you read it, too."

"If you're asking me if Curtis was just being paranoid, I believe the stabbing should answer that question, don't you?"

"I wasn't doubting that he had a right to be suspicious," I said. "I was just wondering what you thought about his list of suspects."

Jeffrey frowned. "Whoever killed him is on that list. I'd swear to it."

"Do you know them very well?"

He just shrugged. "Just from what I've seen from a servant's point of view."

"Is it really all that different from everyone else's?" I asked.

"You have no idea. These people have had money forever, and for the most part, they aren't afraid to show it. Curtis was the rare exception. He never treated me as though I was anything but a friend."

"And the rest of them?"

"Let's just say that I've never gotten used to being treated like a piece of furniture," he said.

"That's terrible," I said.

"Hey, it wasn't *all* bad. I got to hang out with a genuinely nice man and help make the last bit of his life a little easier. There are worse things to do with yourself than that, don't you think?"

"A great many of them," I said. "How are they going to feel about Moose and me barging in on their grief?"

"I doubt that any of them are grieving all that much, but Curtis took care of that. He told them last week that you were his friends and that he'd invited you to stay at the house. I was there when he told them, and trust me, nobody's going to say anything about your presence, at least not to your faces."

"They can whisper behind their backs all that they want," I said with a smile. "It won't be the first time that it's happened to me, and I'm sure that it won't be the last."

Moose came out with a battered old leather overnight bag. Jeffrey got out to take it from him, but my grandfather said, "My arms aren't broken. Pop the trunk and I'll throw it in myself."

Jeffrey smiled. "As much as I appreciate the offer, you might as well get used to being waited on."

"Not a chance, buster," Moose said.

Jeffrey shrugged, and then he did as Moose asked. My grandfather put his bag in the trunk beside mine, and then he slammed the lid for emphasis.

"Home, Jeffrey," he said as he slid into the backseat beside me. He was in a remarkably good mood for a man about to go in search of a killer.

"Buckle up," Jeffrey said.

As we drove to Laurel Landing, I asked my grandfather, "How do you want to play this when we get there?"

"We're friends who've come to stay and pay our respects," Moose said. "Jeffrey told me while you were packing that Curtis has already set it up. When we get there, I suggest that we split up and start asking questions as delicately as we can manage it."

"I'm not thrilled about splitting up from the very start," I said.

"Why not?"

"Moose, we're going to be asking someone who is probably a killer if he murdered our friend."

"Not that openly, I hope," my grandfather said.

"Of course not, but it doesn't mean that the murderer isn't dangerous. Someone killed our friend, and he's asked us to find out who did it."

"We will, Victoria, but I'm not sure how much good it's going to do us to try to plan this. We're going to have to just play it by ear."

"That's what I'm afraid of," I said.

"Come on. It's always worked out in the past," he said with the hint of a smile.

I just wished that I could share it. "All it takes is one bad experience to ruin it all though, isn't that right?"

"You worry too much," Moose said as he looked out the limo window like a little kid.

"Funny, but I think I worry exactly the *right* amount."

"This is an adventure. Let's not forget that," he said.

"It's a job. Let's not forget *that*," I answered.

He turned to me from the window. "You're right. I just don't get enough chances to ride in limousines these days."

As we drove on, I couldn't help wondering who on Curtis's list had the nerve to come into my diner and kill him right under my nose. I had the feeling that my grandfather was whistling past the graveyard. I knew better than to be fooled by his eager demeanor. We'd both been too close to murderers in the past, so we knew what we were getting ourselves into.

At least I hoped we did.

It would be nice having an ally in Jeffrey close by, but I knew that when it came right down to it, Moose and I wouldn't be able to depend on anyone but each other. That was fine with me, though. I knew my grandfather to be a good man when things got dicey, and he knew that he could count on me as well. Since we'd started digging into murder cases that touched our lives, our relationship had changed from family to colleagues. We each had our own strengths that complemented each other, and there was no one else I'd rather be embarking on this quest with but him.

I just hoped that we found Curtis's killer in the time we had allotted to us.

Chapter 4

"Why are we stopping?" I asked Jeffrey half an hour later.

"We're here. Welcome to the Pickle Palace," he said as he paused before driving down the long gravel driveway. The mansion was enormous, and it reminded me more of a European castle than it did a personal residence. There was even a turret on the right edge of the place. The exterior was stone, weathered to a gray patina over the years, and I could see two dozen windows as I looked at the place. The grounds were well kept, which didn't surprise me at all. I couldn't imagine how much money it took to keep this place up, but I had a feeling one month's bill would be more than my total net worth.

"Do you really call it that?" Moose asked as he looked out the window toward the mansion.

"No, its official name is Trane Manor. Pickle Palace is just something the staff calls it. Curtis liked the name himself, but no one else in the family does. He thought that it was a healthy reminder to them all that their fortune was built on pickles. That's why he enjoyed leaving those little plastic pickles everywhere he went."

"So, are we dealing with a bunch of snobs?" I asked.

"On the whole, I'd have to say yes," Jeffrey said. "Are you ready for the grand inquisition?"

"I don't think we'll be that pushy," I said.

"I meant what you are about to get from them. While no one can dispute Curtis's orders to open his home to you, they're all going to want to know more details about your lives than you're probably willing to share. Would you like some free advice worth exactly what it costs?"

"Always," I said.

"If you hear a question that you don't want to answer, just ignore it."

"I do that anyway," Moose said with a smile.

"It's not easy for everybody to do it, but in general, it's a sound policy. If you think of every conversation that you're about to have as a newspaper interview with someone who doesn't believe any comment is off the record, then you'll probably be fine."

I had to laugh. "You paint a rather unflattering picture of them, Jeffrey."

The chauffeur pulled out and started down the long drive. "Just wait. You'll see how right I am."

"How do they feel about you?" I asked.

Jeffrey laughed. "They are mystified as to why a lowly chauffeur has been named executor for Curtis's estate. I've already gotten three bribe attempts to defer the job to one of them."

"Care to share which three offered?" Moose asked.

"If it's all the same to you, I won't. I wouldn't want to see your investigation tainted by any outside sources."

"Fair enough," Moose said.

As we got out of the limo, Moose headed straight for the trunk. "No nonsense from you, Jeffrey. I'll get our bags."

"It's just my job to deliver you here. You'll have to deal with one of the servants about your bags now."

"How many people work here?" I asked as I looked up at the stone columns in front. They were massive, and I wondered how long it must have taken to build the place.

"At last count, there were fourteen," he said, "but that's low. When everyone is in residence, we've had twice that in the past before Curtis got sick."

I couldn't imagine. "Do they all live on-site?"

"They used to, but the only ones here now around the clock are Cassidy, the chef; Humphries, the butler, and me. It's a skeleton crew, but that's the way Curtis wanted it."

The massive front door opened and a dapper older man in a suit walked out to greet us. I was wondering which relative it was when he said, "I'm Humphries. Welcome. If you'll follow me, I'll show you to your rooms."

"Should I get our bags?" Moose asked.

"Stevens will take care of them," Humphries said dismissively. He glanced at Jeffrey, but that was all the acknowledgment that the chauffeur got from the butler. I supposed that being a driver meant that he wasn't worthy of anything more. It felt as though my grandfather and I had just stepped into a Victorian novel. I wasn't at all certain that I'd be able to keep my mouth shut, but then I reminded myself that Moose and I were there for a job, not a party.

"That will be fine," I said as I grabbed Moose's arm and winked at Jeffrey at the same time.

"I'll be around if you need me," Jeffrey said.

"Good," Moose said. "Don't wander off too far."

"I won't," he said.

An older man came out and grabbed the bags, and I worried that he might topple over carrying both of them, though neither Moose nor I had packed all that much. He made it past us with the bags, and Jeffrey closed the trunk before he got in and drove off.

"If you'll both come this way," Humphries said, so we did.

The grand hall was something to see, with dark wood everywhere, broken up only by the paintings, tapestries, fancy rugs, and a frescoed ceiling that was a good twenty feet in the air. It would have made a great basketball court, and I had to wonder what else was in store for us.

As we followed Humphries up the wide staircase to the second floor, I whispered to Moose, "What do you think?"

"I've seen better," he said with a smile.

"Where? At the Biltmore House?" It was a mansion in Asheville built by the Vanderbilts, and Moose and Martha had taken me there for Christmas one year when I'd been a little girl. There were dozens of decorated trees spread throughout the largest private residence in the United States, and I could still remember the splendor of those furnishings. This wasn't on a par with that, but it wasn't all that far behind, either.

At the top of the stairs we made a left, and a little down the hallway, Humphries showed us two rooms side by side. "Mr. Nelson, you're here. Ms. Nelson, you're in the next suite."

"I'm Moose, and this is Victoria," Moose said with a smile as he offered his hand.

Humphries didn't take it, and I had to suppress a grin of my own. If the butler was going to try to outwait my grandfather, he'd better make himself comfortable. After thirty seconds, Humphries looked around surreptitiously, and then he took Moose's hand. "I'm Martin," he said.

"Good to meet you, Martin."

"Sir, you understand that certain things are expected of me," Humphries said.

"I understand, but you also need to know that I'm uncomfortable with anyone waiting on me, and I won't tolerate a deferential attitude."

"In front of the family, I behave as I've been trained to."

"Fair enough, Martin. But when it's just the three of us, I expect you to treat me as an equal."

"I can only do what I can do," Humphries said. I just couldn't bring myself to call him Martin, though Moose didn't seem to have a problem with it.

"Can I call you Marty?" my grandfather asked.

"You may, but don't expect me to answer," the butler said with a smile.

"Got it. Martin, what's the story here?"

"I am not at liberty to discuss my employers, or anything that occurs at Trane Manor." It was clear that Moose had overstepped his bounds.

"I understand, and I won't ask again. Thank you."

"You're most welcome." Humphries showed Moose to his room, and then we went next door to mine. As we did, I said, "I hope you can forgive my grandfather. He doesn't recognize other people's boundaries, nor does the filter between his mouth and his brain always work."

"It's fine," Humphries said. As he opened the door to my

room, I was amazed by how opulent it was. A large four-poster bed was the main focus of the room if you discounted the fireplace, loaded with wood and ready to be lit. There was a thick rug on the stone floor, and a comfortable sitting chair perched beside the broad window that looked over the grounds. "Is there an en suite?" I asked.

"Let me show you," Humphries said as he walked to one of the walls and pressed the center of a wooden panel. The door popped open and revealed a lovely guest bath. "Lark Trane, the founder of the Trane family, loved secret passageways and hidden doorways. This place is riddled with them."

"It must have been a fun place for Curtis to grow up in," I said.

"Actually, Mr. Trane was an unusually serious young man as a youth," Humphries said. I couldn't tell if he approved of his late boss or not.

"Well, I can testify that he turned out to be a warm and welcoming man in the end," I said. "I'm proud to have called him my friend."

"You were lucky to be able to," Humphries said softly. "Now, if there's nothing else, I have work to do."

I'd never been dismissed by a butler before, but hey, there was a first time for everything.

After Humphries was gone, I walked out into the hallway and over to Moose's door. When I tapped lightly on it, he opened it with a smile, and I could see the kid's grin on his face. "Did you ask him about the bathroom?"

"Is yours hidden behind a secret panel, too?" I asked with a grin.

"It's all pretty amazing," Moose said. "I wonder how much this place is worth?"

"Thinking of making an offer?" I asked him, grinning.

"The foyer alone is too rich for my blood," he said. "I don't know about you, but I'm a little hungry. What say we sneak downstairs and see if we can find the kitchen?"

"Shouldn't we ring for Humphries or something?" I asked.

I wasn't sure what the protocol was for this place, but I had a hunch that us wandering around the kitchen and servants' quarters wasn't on the list of things we were allowed to do.

"My, you've become pretty comfortable with calling them servants, haven't you?"

"That's not what I meant, and you know it," I said.

"Take it easy. I was just teasing. Victoria, their rules don't apply to us here. Think about the freedom we have. Curtis gave us the run of the place. We don't have to ask anyone's permission *or* forgiveness. We're here to find his killer, and if that means ignoring the status quo, then so be it."

"You're right," I said with the hint of a laugh. To my surprise, I found that I'd actually been whispering. "I know this isn't a church, or even a library, so why am I acting like it is?"

"It can be overwhelming if you're not used to it," Moose admitted.

"You don't seem to be affected by any of this," I said.

"That's because I've had a great many more years than you have had to learn to laugh at other people's rules. Now let's grab a snack and see if we can do a little investigating while we're at it."

"Lead the way, and I'll follow," I said.

As Moose and I made our way back down the grand staircase, I realized that my grandfather was right. I had to treat this as though it were a regular murder investigation and not some kind of play. Chances were good that someone at the manor had stabbed Curtis right in front of me, robbing him of the last days of his life that he'd been clinging so desperately to. I was glad Moose was with me, for more reasons than I could count.

This was for our friend, and if we ended up upsetting everyone at the Pickle Palace, then so be it. As long as we uncovered Curtis's murderer, I'd be happy with the end results.

Moose was right about something else, too.

I could use a bite to eat myself.

There was some chatter going on in the kitchen when Moose and I finally found it. We should have been issued maps when we got to the house, and honestly, if we hadn't followed our noses, I doubt that we would have found the kitchen at all. The chatting stopped abruptly as the staff noticed us, and it was an uncomfortable silence until Moose asked, "Is there any chance we could get a bite to eat?"

The chef stepped forward. "Dinner will be served promptly at eight."

I glanced at my watch and saw that we had ninety minutes until then. "Is there any way that we could get something to tide us over until then?" I asked.

The chef looked uneasy about how to answer my request. Moose suggested, "We'll take some cheese and crackers if that's all you've got, but seriously, it's not that big a deal."

I didn't know if someone called Humphries, or perhaps there was a secret way to summon the butler, but he hurried into the kitchen before anyone could respond to Moose's request. "If you'll join me outside in the hallway, I'd greatly appreciate it."

I could see that Moose was about to protest, but I didn't want to get any of these people in trouble. "Come on, Moose."

"Victoria, you know how I get when I'm hungry. I'm liable to snap at anyone in sight."

I knew that it was true enough.

Once we were out of the kitchen, I asked, "Humphries, what are the chances we can get something light to snack on?"

"You can have whatever you'd like," the man said. "I need you to go through me, though. We have a specific regimen here, and it would make all of our lives easier if you'd adhere to it."

"Fine," Moose said. "I know when I'm beaten. I'll have a cheese sandwich and a glass of milk."

"What would you like on your sandwich?"

"Cheese and bread," Moose said, and then my grandfather looked at me and asked, "How about you, Victoria?"

"That sounds good to me," I said.

"Very well. If you'll wait in the dining hall, I'll see that you're served immediately."

"I'd be happy to," Moose said with a hint of exasperation in his voice. "If I only knew where exactly it was, or anywhere *else* in this forsaken place."

We really did need to get some food into him. "Don't worry about us. We can find it," I said. "You take care of the food."

Humphries nodded, and then he pointed to the right. "Keep going ten feet, and then take a right. You can't miss it."

"Don't be so sure," I added with a smile. "We've gotten lost before."

"You get used to it after awhile," the chief butler said.

"I don't think we'll have enough of an opportunity to do that," I said. "After all, we'll be gone again in three days."

"True. I'll rejoin you shortly," Humphries said.

Moose started walking, following the directions we'd just gotten, and sure enough, we took the suggested turn and entered the grand dining hall. There were chairs enough for forty diners, and I wondered how often the table was filled with guests since Curtis had taken over. As it was, Moose took a seat at the head of the large, dark oak table, and I grabbed a seat beside him. Place settings had already been set, and I wondered if Moose and I were about to eat cheese sandwiches on the finest china I'd ever seen in my life. A pretty young brunette came a minute later and cleared our settings away, replacing them with less ornate dishes and silverware. It wasn't that the new things weren't fancy; they just weren't as elegant as what had been there before.

Soon enough, our sandwiches and glasses of milk appeared in another minute, and Moose and I shared a bite together in the silence of the large dining room. I was going to have a hard time breaking myself of whispering in the manor. There was just something about the cavernous rooms that suggested I should constantly be aware of the volume of my voice.

"Pretty fancy," I said as I took a bite of my sandwich.

"I don't know. I've had better."

"I wasn't talking about the food. These settings are ritzy."

Moose shrugged. "I don't care if they brought our sandwiches wrapped up in paper towels." He took another big bite and then chased it with a large gulp of milk. "At least the milk's cold."

"I'm pretty happy about that, too," I said as I joined him. "What do you make of all of this?"

"The food, or our surroundings?" my grandfather asked me.

"Enough conversation about the food, okay? I'm talking about Trane Manor."

"I like the name Pickle Palace myself," Moose said with that wicked grin of his.

"That doesn't surprise me in the least, but we should stop calling it that before it gets to be a habit. This place really *is* ostentatious, isn't it?"

Moose finished his sandwich, and then he looked around. "You know, I've never been all that impressed by money," he said. "If I were, I never would have opened a diner."

"I'm glad that you did," I said. "But it's all still really over the top."

"They're just showing off," Moose said, and then he drained his milk. "That hit the spot. It should hold me until dinner, anyway. Who eats at eight o'clock at night, anyway?"

"People who don't have to open a diner at six a.m. the next morning," I said.

"Well, you don't have to worry about that for the next few days. You're on Eastern Pickle Time now," my grandfather said with a broad grin. I knew that it had been dangerous asking him not to constantly refer to the pickle empire that had paid for all that we were surrounded by. It had backfired, and Moose was intentionally working pickles into the conversation. I just hoped that he didn't do it when we started talking to our suspects, but I knew that it was nothing that I could count on. Moose had a mind of his own, and usually I respected him for it, even if it did mean that he was tough to deal with at times. Then again, I'm sure that I had my faults as well. In the end, we were both stubborn, even cantankerous at times. Perhaps it was one of the reasons that we got along so well with each other.

The same brunette returned and whisked our dirty dishes and plates away, and Moose stood. I joined him, and then I asked him, "Where is everyone?"

"They're probably in the secondary master ballroom annex on the third floor," he said with a smile.

"Is there such a place here?" I asked him.

"Who knows? I doubt any of them do," he replied.

"I don't know about you, but I'd like to get started with our interviews," I said as I started back toward the kitchen.

"Where are you going?" Moose asked me.

"I thought I might get some information about the mourners instead of stumbling around blindly from room to room hoping to run across somebody."

"It's not a bad idea, but who are you going to ask?" Moose asked me as he looked around. "This place is so empty it echoes."

"Maybe we can get Humphries on the telephone," I said as I picked one up sitting on a mahogany table tucked into an alcove.

"What are you going to do, dial 0?"

"Why not?" I hit 0, and sure enough, Humphries immediately came on the line.

"May I help you?"

"This is Victoria Nelson," I said. "Where is everyone else?"

"They are gathered in the library waiting for you," he said. "Are you ready to meet them all?"

"Why not?" I asked.

"Excellent. I'll be right with you."

After I hung up, Moose asked, "Did you have any luck?"

"Humphries is on his way. We're going to the library."

Moose shook his head. "Of course we are. Just watch out for Colonel Cody with the crossbow."

"This isn't somebody's twisted idea of a board game, Moose," I said.

"Funny, it surely feels like one," my grandfather said. As we waited for Humphries to appear, my grandfather added, "Can you imagine growing up here? It doesn't seem like a very good fit with the Curtis we knew, does it?"

"Ahem," Humphries said behind us.

"I didn't mean any disrespect by what I just said," Moose explained.

"None was taken," Humphries said with a slight smile. "If you'll follow me, I'll show you to the library."

As we walked behind the butler, Moose looked at me seriously and said, "And so it begins."

Chapter 5

"May I present Moose Nelson and his granddaughter, Victoria Nelson," Humphries announced as he showed us into the book-lined room. I'd always been fascinated by libraries when I'd been a girl, and this place was the stuff that dreams were made of. For starters, it was larger than the home where I now lived. Thousands of leather-bound books lined the room, each carefully tucked into its proper place on the mahogany shelves. There was no room for art here, no tapestries. The volumes *were* the art. Large, comfortable chairs were everywhere, and there was even a broad wooden table near the fireplace, with seating for an even dozen.

Just five places were taken at the moment, though.

I was surprised to see that Jeffrey occupied one of them, and I smiled at him. He nodded in return, but he didn't speak.

"May I present Sarah Harper, Tristan Wellborne, Christopher Crane, and Charlotte Trane. You've met Jeffrey already," Humphries said. As he spoke each name, the person in question offered us a nod, but no more. Sarah Harper looked to be somewhere in her mid-twenties. She was wearing a wispy dress that accentuated her slight figure, and she might be called pretty in the right light, but this clearly wasn't it. Her front teeth were a little too prominent, and her forehead a bit too broad. Tristan was a few years older, wearing a casual shirt and slacks that both fit him snugly. What Sarah lacked in looks, Tristan made up for double. He was handsome, even devilishly so, and from his grin, I knew that he would be trouble to any woman who might catch his fancy. Christopher Crane, somewhere in his mid-sixties, was wearing a three-piece suit, and from the way he carried himself, I wondered if he slept in it as well. That left Charlotte Trane, Curtis's sister. She must have been his younger sister, because I doubted that she was much past sixty herself. She wore a suit as well, and from her demeanor, I was guessing that she was always business, all of the time.

Moose and I knew who we were dealing with now, but we still needed a program to tell us how each of them was connected to Curtis other than his sister, Charlotte. I was still trying to figure out how to learn what their relationships were when Moose spoke up beside me. “We were two of the last people on earth that Curtis befriended,” he said. “My granddaughter and I have come here to learn more about him, and I hope that you’ll indulge us.” Moose winked at me, and then he added, “Curtis encouraged us to write about him recently, since he knew that Victoria and I have had some success in the past.”

This was news to me, and I wondered how long Moose had been holding onto that particular ploy. I had to admire the cover story. It would certainly allow us to ask some rather nosy questions as we tried to get to the bottom of Curtis’s murder. What credentials did we have, though? Maybe no one would ask.

“Pardon me for asking, but what makes you qualified to do that?” Charlotte Trane asked pointedly.

Moose hadn’t been expecting it, but I’d had a moment to consider our options. “We write under a pseudonym,” I said. “It’s all very hush-hush, so I’m afraid that we aren’t allowed to say more than that. The nondisclosure agreements publishers use these days are really pretty dreadful.”

My grandfather nodded his approval of my addition to his story. “That explains why Curtis wanted us here, but what brings you all to the table?”

A few of them looked shocked that he had the nerve to even ask that kind of question, but Moose was bold, and he knew that if he kept quiet, someone would start talking, if only to fill the silence. I knew better than to interrupt him myself. I’d studied at his knee, and I liked to think on my best day that I was his equal, though I was probably just kidding myself.

Finally, Sarah broke the silence. "Of course. You know Jeffrey; he brought you here. For some reason, my uncle placed a great deal of trust in him, and he is acting as executor of the estate."

Jeffrey waved and offered a slight smile, but again, he didn't speak. Sarah went on. "This is my older brother, Tristan, or Tris, if you like."

"I prefer Tristan, actually," the young man said, and as he did, he smiled broadly at me. Wow. I was a happily married woman, but I'd still have to fortify myself against this man's charms.

"Are you really brother and sister?" Moose asked. "I'm just curious because you have different last names."

"Alas, I had the misfortune to be wed to Nathaniel Harper once upon a time," Sarah said. "The mistake was corrected quickly enough, but I found that I enjoyed being a Harper, so I kept it."

"You are both Tranes, no matter what else might be true about you," Charlotte said. "You have Trane blood in you, proud and noble blood."

Christopher Crane raised a finger. "I don't have any Trane blood in me, but don't hold it against me. I was Curtis's financial planner, closest advisor, and dearest friend." He said it as though he were reading it off of an index card, and I didn't believe that the last part was true under any circumstances.

I could see one problem right away.

Every last one of them was tall and thin.

That meant that I had to strike one theory out on the face of it. I'd hoped to eliminate at least one of our suspects based on sheer size alone, but these folks all fit the basic parameters of the mysterious killer who'd struck so effectively at the diner.

"Now that we've dispensed with the formalities, I suggest we get on with this," Charlotte said. "I'm sure that my brother had his reasons for inviting you here, and we'll extend every courtesy to you both as guests, but I ask that you stay in your rooms at night and not wander through the hallways unescorted."

Why was that? Was she warning us, or was it an outright threat? What did she have to hide? It just made me want to go exploring even more after everyone else was asleep, but I decided to keep that inclination to myself.

Charlotte continued, "Now, if you'll excuse me, I'll see to our supper. We'll speak later, I'm sure."

"I'm sure we will," Moose said, echoing her sentiment.

It was clear that Charlotte was used to getting the last word in every conversation, and just as certain to me that she'd met her match in my grandfather.

After Charlotte was gone, Crane said, "I'd appreciate it if we could chat first. I have other obligations, after all." As he said the last bit, he looked directly at Sarah and Tristan, and I wondered about the relationship between them. There was obviously some animosity there. The real question was if any of them would talk to us about it.

"Would you three mind waiting outside?" I asked Sarah, Tristan, and Jeffrey. "This shouldn't take long, but we'd like to do it on an individual basis."

"Why on earth could that possibly matter?" Sarah asked. She seemed quite put off by the suggestion that we had the nerve to ask her to leave, and I suspected that we might have a problem getting rid of her. Tristan stepped in, though. "Come along, dear sister. After all, this is our uncle's last request. Who are we not to honor it?"

She left, albeit reluctantly, and Jeffrey followed suit. I didn't have a pad of paper with me, or even a pen. How were we supposed to take notes? I knew that we weren't really writing a tribute to Curtis, but we had to at least make it look as though we were. Again, Moose stepped in. He reached into his pocket and pulled out a small spiral notebook with a pen attached. It was the pad he used to take notes to remind him of things, not that he was getting old and feeble, but rather because his mind *always* seemed to take off in a dozen different directions at the same time, and if he didn't write it all down, some of it would be lost forever.

"How long did you know Curtis, Christopher?" Moose asked the man as we sat down across from him at the table.

"Please, call me Crane. Everyone does."

"Fine then," Moose said. "When did you two first meet?"

"We went to prep school together," Crane said. "Our friendship was based on two odd young men paired together by a dean who couldn't be bothered with us. We clicked, and we've been friends ever since."

"And yet you worked for him?" I asked. I was friends with all of the employees at The Charming Moose. As a matter of fact, I was related to most of them, but that didn't mean that they didn't know who was boss when they were at the diner, and that included my grandfather. I couldn't imagine having my own best friend, Rebecca Davis, working for me.

"I took the position with some reluctance, but he needed my help, and I couldn't say no. I'm sure that you understand."

I was sure that I didn't, but I decided not to get into that at the moment. "How did you two get along towards end?" Moose asked him.

"The same as always," Crane said lightly. "Curtis and I had no problem mixing business with pleasure, and I'm pleased to be able to say that I was able to make his life easier, especially at the end."

"Why at the end in particular?" I asked him. There was more to this story than he was giving us. "You can be candid with us, Crane. You need to tell us everything out of respect to your friendship with Curtis. It's what he wanted, remember?" I hoped that Curtis's spirit would forgive me for taking the liberties that I was taking, but he'd asked us to solve his murder, so I hoped that he wouldn't have minded me stretching the truth a little.

"I'm surprised that he didn't share that with you, if you were as close as you've claimed," Crane said. "His entire family was unhappy with him. They didn't accept Curtis's plan to get rid of his money, and I've got a suspicion that one of them had something to do with what happened to him."

Chapter 6

"What!" Moose said, doing a credible job of feigning ignorance. "You actually think that one of *them* might have killed him?"

"The man certainly didn't stab himself," Crane said. "It's not as outrageous as you might think. He was just about to sign the new will when someone killed him. I understand people commit murder for a great deal less than a hundred million dollars."

Wow, Curtis really *did* have money.

Moose whistled. "That offers a great *many* incentives, doesn't it?"

"It used to be quite a bit more than that, but Curtis was dispensing it quietly for quite a while before anyone caught on to what he was doing. He set up a dummy account in order to give his money away, and it took them some time to see what he was doing."

"How long did it take *you*?" I asked him softly.

"Not all that long, but since I didn't have a stake in it, I kept the information to myself. I worked for Curtis—no one else."

That was odd. Jeffrey had said basically the same thing earlier. "Was he truly that good a boss?"

"He was indeed, and a good friend, as well. I'll miss him."

"What will happen to you now?" I asked.

"I'll see this through, and then I'll most likely take the modest retirement I've been promising myself for years. I've managed to save up a nice little nest egg, and I've got an acre in the mountains near Asheville that I spend much too little time enjoying. I'm not afraid to admit that seeing what happened to Curtis has been a wake-up call for me. I'm not going to spend the rest of my life working for someone else."

"I can respect that," Moose said. "Since I retired, I've never been so busy."

I decided to let that one slide, since one of the things Moose did these days was help me in my murder investigations, as well as pitching in at the diner's grill whenever I needed him.

"If you were to pick *one* of them out as a cold-blooded killer, which one would it be?" I asked him.

Crane frowned. "That's an odd topic for a tribute to him, isn't it?"

"Think about how dramatic it will be if we supply Curtis's killer in the closing chapter," I said, making it up as I went along.

"Yes, I can see where he would have appreciated that," Crane said with a slight smile. He rubbed his chin for a few moments, and then the financial manager finally said, "If I had to guess, I'd say that it most likely was Charlotte. It could be because I've never liked her, or trusted her, either. Then again, Tristan isn't a bad place to start, either." Crane glanced at his watch, and then he stood abruptly. "I'm sorry, but that's all the time I have right now. I'll be back later tonight though, so if you want to continue our conversation, we can do so then."

"Do you live here on the grounds?" Moose asked him.

"No, I'm just a guest here for the next few days, the same as you two are."

"How about the others?" I asked.

"Charlotte has a home on the property next to this. It's so grand that it makes this place look like the gardener's quarters."

"Do Sarah and Tristan live with her?" Moose asked.

"No, but they visit quite often. They're staying *here* at the moment, though. Curtis insisted. I heard that even Charlotte might stay. How cozy that will be for all of us." Crane paused at the door, but before he opened it, he asked me, "Shall I send in your next interviewee?"

"That would be great," I said.

"Which one would you like?"

"Like you said earlier, since Charlotte is busy, Tristan might not be a bad place to start."

Crane grinned at that. "I'll tell him that it's his turn. Good luck. I truly hope that you catch the killer. Curtis deserved better than he got."

"What can I possibly tell you about my uncle that isn't already public knowledge?" Tristan asked as he walked into the library thirty seconds after the financial planner left. There was a smug arrogance to the man, an outright cockiness that gave weight to his words. He thought that he was important, and so help me, he managed to convey it to us without the slightest effort.

"How did you two get along?" I asked him.

He gave me that dazzling smile, but I wasn't going to bite. "Famously," he said. "Why wouldn't we? After all, we were kindred spirits."

From what little I knew of Curtis, I doubted that most sincerely.

"How so?" Moose asked.

I noticed that Tristan's smile wasn't nearly as bright for my grandfather as it had been for me. "We both loved life and tried to get the most of it in the end."

"I know that your uncle had the means to indulge any whim he might have had, but what about you, Tristan?"

"Pardon me?" he asked Moose. His tone was one of astonishment, as though it was impossible for him to imagine someone prying into his life so personally.

"He wants to know how much money you have," I supplied. I smiled at him this time, but I made certain that there wasn't an ounce of warmth in it. The quicker he realized that he couldn't charm me, the better it was for our investigation.

"I'm comfortable," Tristan said.

"Me, too. The temperature is just right," Moose said. "Don't change the subject. Have you relied on money from your family all of your life?"

"I won't answer that," Tristan said petulantly.

Moose shrugged, and as he scribbled into his notebook, he said aloud, "Tristan Wellborne, most likely broke and living off relatives."

"I resent that," Tristan said.

"I don't blame you," I said. "I can't imagine not working for a living myself."

"I'll have you know that I'm a very successful artist known in many corners of the art world."

"Oh, really?" I asked. "Which corners are those?"

"Watercolor and oil abstracts are currently my specialty," he said.

"Interesting," I said. "Have you ever been accepted into any juried shows? Which societies do you belong to? Who have you studied under?" I'd had a customer at the diner a few months before, a jovial heavyset older woman who came in with paint splattered on her hands and clothes during every visit. It turned out that she was a traveling artist on retreat, and we'd had some fascinating conversations while she'd been in town. It was only after she left Jasper Fork that I'd looked her up online and found that she was famous in her field.

Tristan waved a hand dismissively in the air. "None of that really matters. What counts is the fire of inspiration, the execution of brush to canvas, and imagination. I'm ahead of my time."

"I'm sure that you are," I said. I had a hunch that Tristan would have been lucky to be able to afford his paints with his income as an artist, let alone support himself. "Still, it's a tough way to make a living."

"I'll admit that I've had patrons from time to time," he said. "People who truly appreciate fine art."

"Do you happen to be related to any of them?" I asked.

"I won't answer that," Tristan said.

"That sounds like a yes to me," Moose said as he scribbled more into his notebook.

"Where were you when your uncle was murdered?" I asked him. "We don't need the police to supply a time of death, since I saw it happen myself."

"I was in my studio painting, as a matter of fact."

"Can anyone confirm that?" I asked.

"Of course not. When I'm entertaining my muse, I don't allow anyone to disturb me. It's a commune with the spirits."

"Sure," Moose said. "So that's a big no, right?"

Tristan stood. "I've indulged this farce long enough. I'm leaving."

He stood there glaring at each of us in turn, as though he was defying us to try to stop him. I didn't have any interest in doing that at all. Frankly, the man was giving me a headache.

"One last thing," Moose asked before the artist left.

"What is it?" Tristan asked.

"If you didn't kill your uncle, who do you think did?"

Before he answered, Tristan got the most wicked grin on his face that I'd ever seen in my life. "You'll have to ask Sarah that."

"Your *sister*?" I asked. Was he really throwing his own family member under the bus?

"She's the only Sarah I know who had a beef with my uncle. All I know is that they were fighting about money a few days ago, and today he's dead. What do you think?"

"I think we'd like to speak with her next," I said. "Send her in on your way out."

"I'd be delighted to," he said, and then Tristan left us, being sure to leave the door wide open after he walked out.

I whispered to my grandfather, "Can you believe this guy?"

"He's a prince among men, isn't he?" Moose asked with a wicked little grin of his own. "That doesn't make him a killer, though."

"I'm starting to feel really sorry for Curtis," I said.

Moose looked around. "I'm not there yet myself. Sure,

he had a screwed-up family, but who doesn't? At least he had all of that money to comfort him."

"Do you think that *we're* messed up?" I asked my grandfather.

"No, not us. We're the exception to the rule. Our family has *always* been perfectly normal. Don't you agree?"

I had to laugh. Leave it to Moose to make me smile at a time like that, but I'd meant what I'd said. Curtis deserved better, and I had to wonder if having money offered him any solace in the end.

Sarah walked in, or floated, if I were to describe it more vividly. She looked frail in her wispy dress, and I wondered for a moment if she had the strength to kill her uncle. Then I realized that if the placement of that metal stake was just right, it wouldn't take an impossible amount of strength to do it.

"So, we hear that you were fighting with your uncle about money just before he died," Moose said. That was my grandfather, jumping right into the fray. Sometimes I wondered about his direct approach, but not now. Sarah's smile was extinguished quickly as her face contorted. "My brother is a liar and a thief," she said. "If he tells you that it's raining outside, I wouldn't reach for an umbrella if I were you. Did he say that I was fighting with Uncle Curtis?"

Moose shrugged. "I'd rather not reveal our sources of information," he said. "That way you can feel confident about what you tell us."

"Shout it from the rooftop if you'd like. I don't care. Tristan was a little leech, and when Uncle Curtis finally cut him off, I thought he was going to go for the man's throat right there on the spot."

It appeared that these siblings were also bloodthirsty rivals. This was going to be interesting.

"Does that mean that Curtis was his art patron, his angel, so to speak?" I asked.

"My uncle supported him financially for years until it became clear that my brother's sole talent was getting money from him."

"You don't care for your brother's art then?" I asked.

She shook her head. "No one, and I mean no one, calls what Tristan does art. I'm certain that a child could do better, an untalented one at that. Sure, I indulge him by posing for him from time to time, but I know that it's all just a colossal waste of time."

"Would you mind elaborating on the fight you had with Curtis?" Moose asked.

"There's really nothing much to tell," Sarah said.

"Then it won't take long," I replied. "We've got time."

She thought about denying our request, but finally Sarah shook her head and spoke. "I asked him for a loan, okay? It wasn't much, and I knew that he could easily afford it, but he turned me down cold. I got angry, and I told him so."

"How much are we talking about here?" I asked.

"Twenty thousand measly dollars," she said. "Can you imagine? I would have paid him back at the end of the month when my stipend came through from my trust, but he wouldn't do it."

"Did he give you a reason why he said no?" I asked.

She looked as though she were about to stamp her foot before she spoke. "He told me that I needed to learn to budget my expenses better. I'm living as frugally as I can, but twenty thousand dollars a month just doesn't seem to last until I get more."

I couldn't help myself; I laughed long and hard, and Moose caught the fever and began to chuckle himself.

"What's so funny?" Sarah asked belligerently.

"You poor thing," I said. "I know people who would kill for that kind of money."

Moose followed that statement up with a question. "Would you, Sarah?"

"What? No, of course not. My trust has nothing to do with my uncle. It was set up by my grandfather. Tristan gets the same amount, and he *always* runs out of money before I do."

"Do you have an alibi for the time of the murder?" I asked.

"I don't know," she said.

"How can you not know?" Moose asked. "It was today!"

"Don't yell at me," she said in a hurt voice that I was certain worked on many men.

Just not my grandfather.

"Where were you, Sarah?"

"Well, I wasn't anywhere near your *diner*, that's for sure," she said. "I was tied up somewhere else."

"I'm afraid that we're going to need something more concrete than that," I told her.

"I'm sorry, but right now, that's all that I care to say."

"You're not being very cooperative; you know that, don't you?" Moose asked her.

"I just lost someone I loved dearly. Answering your questions isn't a priority for me after the horror of losing my uncle." She started to cry then, big crocodile tears that I didn't buy for one second. "It's too painful for me. I can't go on." Sarah rushed out of the room, and I was certain that we'd just seen a performance instead of a display of her true emotions.

"What did you just say to my niece?" Charlotte asked us both twenty seconds later. "She ran out of here in tears. I won't have you disturbing my family in this tragic time, do you understand me?"

"We have to find the truth," I said.

"For a biography that no one is ever going to read?" the matron asked sharply.

"We're not doing this for anyone but your brother," Moose said. "Profit is not our motive here."

"Then you fit right in with the rest of my family. I'm the only one left with any sense of responsibility for the money our ancestors acquired. Curtis was a solid businessman for many years, but I'm afraid that his illness tainted his ability to focus on what was important."

"And what would that be?" I asked.

"Our bloodline, of course," she said.

"So, who do you think might have killed him?" Moose asked her.

"Why do you believe that I have any idea of who that might be?" she asked.

"Because I've watched you assess those around you as though you were weighing them on your very own set of scales, and I have a hunch that they've all come up short in your eyes."

It was fascinating. I could see her considering her options as she tried to decide how to react. To my surprise, her response was a slight smile. "Remind me never to play poker with you. Yes, I admit that I *have* given it a great deal of thought."

"Have you come up with any conclusions?" Moose asked her.

"I don't trust Crane. Actually, I never really have."

"Has he done anything to earn your suspicion besides not being related directly to you?" Moose asked.

"That's a fair question," Charlotte said, "but I don't have an answer, at least not yet. I'll find the truth though; you can trust me on that."

"Were you and your brother close?" I asked her. I hoped that they'd at least had a better relationship than the next generation appeared to have had with him.

"We were, once upon a time," she said, "but his illness finally drove us apart. He changed in more ways than I can describe. Things that were once important to him became nothing in his eyes, while he became odder and odder. I suppose you know about those ridiculous plastic pickles he loved to give out."

"I thought they were charming," I said, and it was true. It had made Curtis stand out, something that was nearly always good in my mind.

"It was an embarrassment," she said abruptly. "Our family has owned many businesses over the years, gradually building up into an empire. Certainly our people sold pickles a long time ago, but we've grown into a huge corporation."

"But the brunt of your fortune still started making and selling pickles, right?" I asked. It had been a point of pride with Curtis about his humble beginnings, and I hated seeing his sister trash the image.

"It hardly matters at this point," she said. "I must ask you both to restrain yourselves from asking such personal questions while you're guests here. It's unseemly."

"Maybe it is," I said, "but it was what Curtis wanted. Just because it makes you uncomfortable is not enough reason for us to stop."

"Must I remind you that you both are here at *my* discretion?" she asked.

"Actually, Jeffrey is the one who has control of the estate right now," Moose said. "I'll bet *that* was a real surprise for you all."

"It just shows you how much my brother had slipped in the last year of his life. I'm afraid that Jeffrey is in it well over his head."

"Then we'll be here to help him if he needs it," I said.

"So then, you are on *his* side in all of this," she said curtly.

"As a matter of fact, the *only* reason that we're here is because of Curtis," I answered. "We aren't going anywhere."

"So be it," she said as there was a knock on the door.

Before Moose or I could answer, Charlotte called out, "Enter."

Humphries walked in. "Dinner is being served in the grand dining hall."

"We'll be there shortly," she said, and Humphries backpedaled out of the room quickly. Before Charlotte would allow us to leave, she turned to my grandfather and me. "This conversation about how you two are treating my family isn't over."

"Maybe not, but it's at least going to be postponed. That snack wasn't enough to hold me. I'm starving."

“Then follow me,” she said.

Charlotte led the way, with Moose following close behind, and me taking up the rear. As we walked toward the grand dining room, I couldn’t help feeling a little sorry for Curtis, despite the opulent surroundings. Everyone, with the exception of Jeffrey, had just accused someone else in his inner circle of murder, and I had to wonder if we pushed Jeffrey hard enough, he’d supply a favorite as well.

All in all, it wasn’t a very auspicious exit for such a fine man.

Chapter 7

We didn't fill much of the expansive table once we were all seated, but I was happy to see that everyone was present and accounted for, including Jeffrey. He looked as though he felt out of place sitting at the table with the family, something that was reinforced when he spoke. "Charlotte, as I said before, I'd be happy to eat in the kitchen. It's what I'm used to."

"Nonsense," the matriarch said. "My brother elevated your position from chauffeur to executor. I'm afraid that there's no going back now. You will dine with us, as is due your new position."

"For goodness sake, Aunt Charlotte, if he's more comfortable eating with the help, then let the poor man go," Tristan said. I knew that he wasn't saying it to help Jeffrey, but to satisfy his own desire to have the past order preserved at the table.

"I simply will not allow it," Charlotte said. The withering glare she gave Tristan would have been enough to melt a lesser man, but it just bounced right off of him. "Let's speak of it no more."

The china and stemware were all very elegant, but the first thing I noticed was the small brass bell beside Charlotte's plate. I couldn't believe it when she actually picked it up and rang it. Sure enough, one of the servers came out of the kitchen carrying a heavily laden tray of shrimp cocktail and assorted fruit cups. She knew without asking what each member of the family wanted, and Jeffrey was no surprise to her either, since she winked at him discreetly as she placed a fruit cup in front of him without asking. Moose and I were another matter, though. My grandfather chose the shrimp while I chose the fruit. My allergy to seafood made the choice an easy one.

I took my first bite, and I wasn't the least bit surprised to find the blueberry delicious. There was no doubt that this family spared no expense when it came to pampering themselves. I had to wonder if that had been the case when Curtis had been in residence, but it was certainly that way now.

Charlotte took a dainty bite of her shrimp, and then she addressed my grandfather and me. "We ordinarily don't have cocktails with our evening meal, but if it's your practice, we'll be more than happy to provide you with whatever you'd like."

"Thank you, but water is fine with me," I said.

"Do you have any single malt whisky on hand?" Moose asked. I knew that he rarely drank at home, so his request surprised me.

"Certainly," she said, and the bell was rung again. Moose requested his drink neat, and soon the brunette server named Margo showed up with a small glass of amber liquid. My grandfather studied it in the light, took a deep breath as he swirled it in the glass, and then he took a small sip. The smile that spread across his face made me wish that I'd asked for one as well, but it was too late now.

"Is it to your taste?" Charlotte asked him.

"It's perfect," Moose said. "I'd propose a toast to Curtis's memory, but it's bad luck to salute someone with just water." He stood, raised his glass dramatically, and then my grandfather said, "To Curtis Trane, one of the better men that I've ever had the privilege of knowing."

After he drank, my grandfather sat back down. I'd looked around the table as Moose made the sentimental gesture, and I saw a smile from Jeffrey, but the others were clearly unimpressed.

Soon enough, the appetizer was replaced by cold vichyssoise soup.

"Cook is off his game tonight," Sarah said after she took a small sip of the soup.

"I think it's delicious," I said.

"You clearly aren't used to the level of perfection we expect here," Sarah said, almost as though she was speaking in sympathy. "You run a truck stop; is that right?"

"It's the best diner in our part of North Carolina," Moose said. For a moment I thought he was going to leave his seat he was so upset, but I put a hand on his shoulder and he settled back down.

"Of course. Forgive me," Sarah said. "What type of fare do you normally serve there?"

"You name it, and we can make it," I replied.

It was pretty clear that she doubted that with all of her heart, but I wasn't about to let her get under my skin. "What is it exactly that *you* do, Sarah?"

She looked at me defiantly. "I'm a student of life."

"Wow, what does *that* pay?" Moose asked.

"Everything in this world is not about money," Sarah snapped.

Moose wasn't about to back down, though. "It can be if you don't have any, but then I'm not talking to anyone who's ever felt that way, am I?"

Charlotte stepped in before things got any bloodier. "Could we all strive to be more civil to each other, particularly during this meal? Let's try to focus on the good memories we've all had of my brother. We at least owe him that. Agreed?"

The family nodded their assents readily enough, and Jeffrey added his as well. Moose and I really didn't have much choice to agree without looking heartless and uncaring. It was a clever move on Charlotte's part, and I had to wonder if she had prompted her niece to goad us into an argument so she could use it against us.

After that, enveloped in idle chitchat that did nothing to advance our investigation, we had an excellent roast with baby carrots and new potatoes that I wished my husband could have tasted. The cook had used an unusual spice combination on the roast's rub, and I knew that Greg would have been able to identify every ingredient. After that, we had light and crispy salads, and then dessert and coffee. The chocolate truffles were amazing, but I restrained myself and didn't clear the tray, as difficult as it was for me to do.

"That was wonderful," I told Charlotte after the meal was completed. "Would it be appropriate for me to give my compliments to the chef?"

"Don't praise him too much," Sarah said. "I still believe that the soup was a bit bland."

"It was fine, Sarah," Tristan said.

"What do you know about the art of good food?" she asked. It was clear that the tiptoeing part of our evening was over. "Or good art of *any* kind?"

"I'm warning you," Tristan said before Charlotte spoke up.

"Enough." The single word was enough to get them to agree to a reluctant truce.

Jeffrey took the opportunity to say, "If you'll excuse us, I need to go over some reports with Crane tonight."

"It's not all about business, young man," Charlotte said.

"Not always, but this *is* important," Crane said. He turned to Jeffrey and suggested, "Let's go into the study and work where we won't disturb anyone."

"That would be fine," Jeffrey said. "I'll meet you there in a few minutes."

"You're not coming with me?" Crane asked.

"I need to have a word in private with Moose and Victoria first," he said.

It was clear that Crane wasn't thrilled with the prospect of being kept waiting by a chauffeur and two commoners from a diner, but he really didn't have much choice in the matter. "Don't be too late," he said. "I'm not a young man anymore."

"I won't be long," he said.

"If you'll excuse us," Jeffrey said.

"Of course," Charlotte replied. "I'd like a word with Tristan and Sarah myself. Come along, you two."

They weren't pleased about that, but they obeyed

nonetheless, and we had the dining room to ourselves. Once they were all gone, Jeffrey grinned at us. "Welcome to the zoo."

"I'd say that it's more like a circus if you asked me," Moose said, not even trying to keep his voice in check. "Does *anybody* here miss Curtis?"

"The three of us do," Jeffrey said. "I'm sorry I didn't join you in your toast, but I still can't get used to the idea that these people are treating me as though I'm an equal all of a sudden after all of these years of being looked down upon."

"You missed out, my friend," Moose said. "That's the best whisky I've had since I was in Ireland, and that's saying something." My grandfather had taken an extended trip there before opening The Charming Moose, and though he'd only stayed a week, he'd made a lifetime of memories.

"Next time," Jeffrey said. "Have you had any luck so far?"

I wasn't sure that we should be sharing with him just yet, especially since our investigation had just started. I tried to warn Moose off from talking about it, but I couldn't get his attention. "We're doing what we can," he said, and I nodded in approval of his brevity.

Jeffrey smiled apologetically. "I don't mean to push you, but in less than three days, *all* of us will be out of here. You need to work as quickly as you can."

"We're giving it our full attention," I said. "Do you really have reports to go over with Crane tonight, or were you just trying to break up our charming little dinner party?"

"I'm not an idiot by any stretch of the imagination, but Curtis's estate is complicated. What made him think that *I* could handle it?"

"He trusted you," I said as I put a hand on his shoulder. "I'm certain that he cared more about that than any qualifications you might be lacking."

"I understand that, and it does mean something to me, but I wish I had someone besides Crane helping me. After all, he's got to be a suspect, right?"

"He is," I said.

"You know, you don't have to do this all on your own," Moose said after a momentary pause.

"Are you volunteering?" Jeffrey asked.

"Not me," Moose said quickly. "But I do know a woman who could lend you a hand."

"You're not talking about Judge Dixon, are you?" I asked. Holly Dixon may or may not have had a fling with my grandfather once upon a time, and my grandmother still didn't trust the woman all these years later.

"No, of course not. I'm talking about asking Renee to pitch in." Renee West was a customer at the diner, a forensic accountant who specialized in complicated cases.

"That's brilliant," I said, and then I turned to Jeffrey. "I'm sure that she's not cheap, but you won't find anyone any better."

"Money's not an issue," Jeffrey said. "I've got a discretionary fund that you wouldn't believe. Do you trust her?"

"I do," Moose said, and I echoed the sentiment.

"That's good enough for me, then. I suppose the next question is if she'll take it on."

"If Moose calls her, I'm sure of it. She's sweet on him."

"She's no such thing," Moose said in a stammer. "She's just a child, Victoria."

"A thirty-one-year-old divorcée is not a child, Moose."

"Compared to me? You'd better believe that she is."

"Would you mind calling her for me tomorrow, Moose?" Jeffrey asked.

"Why wait until then? I'll call her right now."

"Do you have her home number?" I asked him with a grin.

"No, but I've got her cell number on my phone," he said, waiting for a remark from me. I decided that I'd teased him enough for one night.

As Moose spoke in a hushed whisper, Jeffrey said to me, "I appreciate everything that you two are doing, Victoria. Curtis would have been pleased."

"We're happy to help," I said. "How are you holding up? After all, you just lost a dear friend. It's got to be especially tough dealing with all of these details."

"Honestly, I'm thankful to have it. It's letting me take my mind off what happened to Curtis. I'm sure that it will hit me soon enough, but for now, I have a reason to keep it together." He paused, and then Jeffrey added, "I admit that I just about lost it when Moose paid tribute to Curtis at dinner, though."

"Join the club," I said. "Even if it *was* just the two of us. What's wrong with those people? They were supposed to be the closest folks in the world to Curtis, but I didn't see any sign of it in there."

"If it's any consolation, I've never gotten it, either," he said as Moose hung up and rejoined us.

"Great news. She just finished up an audit, so she's free. She'll be here in half an hour."

The relief on Jeffrey's face was obvious. "I don't know how to thank you."

"She's the one to thank," Moose said. "You're in good hands with Renee."

"I'm sure that I am," Jeffrey said. "I'd better go break the news to Crane. I'm sure that he's going to be upset about it."

"Why is that?" I asked.

"He wants to spoon-feed this to me, but I'm not entirely sure that I trust him," Jeffrey said with a hint of hesitation in his voice.

"Do you think that *he* might have killed Curtis?" I asked.

"I don't know. I can't say that one way or the other, but *something's* going on with him; I'm sure of it. It will be great getting Ms. West's input."

"Do yourself a favor and don't ever call her that to her face," I said. "She's Renee, plain and simple."

"Moose, we both know that there's nothing plain about Renee." She was a quite nice looking woman, and she had an electric personality, too. Her divorce had been a bitter one, and as far as I knew, she hadn't dated since it had been finalized, but you never knew. Maybe she and Jeffrey would hit it off.

"She's okay," he said, barely able to hide his smile. My grandfather patted Jeffrey's arm. "You're in for a treat, my friend."

"I just hope that she can help me," the executor replied.

"I'll let you know when she gets here," I said.

"I'd appreciate that," Jeffrey said.

After he left to rejoin Crane, it was back to just Moose and me.

"I want to text Renee and have her call me when she gets here," I said.

"I don't mind phoning her back," Moose answered.

"I'm sure you don't, but this will just take a second. Give me her number."

After I finished sending the text, I put my phone away and asked my grandfather, "Do you have any ideas about what we can do in the meantime?"

"I think we should follow through with your suggestion that we should congratulate the chef," Moose said.

"And poke around behind the scenes while we're at it?" I asked.

My grandfather smiled broadly at me. "If we uncover anything while we're talking to the staff, I admit that I wouldn't be unhappy about it."

"Then let's go have ourselves a chat with the help," I said.

"You're not going to call them that, are you?" Moose asked as we made our way toward the kitchen.

"Of course not. We've got something in common with them, though. We've all worked for a living, which is more than I can say about most of the people we're dealing with here."

"Let's make sure that they know that," Moose said.

"Do you think it will help our cause?" I asked.

"Well, as far as I'm concerned, it couldn't hurt," he replied.

Chapter 8

"Excuse me," I said to the group of workers as Moose and I walked into the kitchen. "May we speak with the chef?"

"Is there a problem?" a beefy young man in whites holding a meat cleaver asked me.

"On the contrary," Moose said with a hearty smile. "That beef rub was unbelievable. Was that sage I tasted?"

"Among other things," the man said as he put the cleaver down. "Nice catch."

"I've jockeyed a grill or two in my time, though nothing on your level," my grandfather said as he extended a hand. "My name's Moose, and this is Victoria."

The chef took it, and I saw that he and Moose were locked in a struggle to see who could apply the most pressure. Evidently it was a draw, because when they broke, both men were happy enough with the results. "I'm Cassidy," he said.

"Pleasure to meet you. We were wondering if you had a few minutes. We're guests here for the next few days."

"I know who you are," Cassidy said. He looked around and saw that the three other people cleaning up the kitchen were watching us. "Get back to work. There's nothing to see here."

Moose said, "We're talking with everyone about Curtis," he said, "and we were wondering if you had any insights about what happened to him in the end."

"It's tough," Cassidy said. "There's not much to say. We all worked for him; we weren't his pals." It was clear that the chef didn't really want to discuss his former employer, and I couldn't blame him. Most likely *everyone* was going to be out of work soon, and it didn't make sense to risk future employment.

"We understand," I said. "Come on, Moose."

My grandfather looked surprised when I suggested that we

leave so soon, but I had my reasons.

Once we were alone out in the hallway again, Moose asked me, "What was that all about? I was just getting warmed up."

"It was obvious that Cassidy wasn't going to say anything, but did you notice the young woman washing dishes? She's the one who served us tonight, too. I think her name was Margo. Anyway, she looked like she was dying to say something when we asked Cassidy about Curtis."

"No, I missed that," Moose said with a bit of grudging respect in his voice. "How are we going to get her off by herself so we can speak with her?"

"Let's find Jeffrey. He might be able to help," I said.

"I hate to bother him," my grandfather said. "He's up to his eyebrows in work right now."

"Maybe so," I replied, "but we need his help navigating the treacherous waters around here." My phone rang, and I answered it quickly.

"I'm out front," Renee said.

"We'll be right there," I said. "Come on," I told Moose as I put my phone away. "Renee's here."

We walked down the hall, and I saw Humphries lingering near the front door. "We've got this, Humphries," I said.

"As you please," he said, though he clearly wasn't happy about being usurped from his job.

I opened the door and found Renee standing there in burgundy slacks and a lovely blouse. It was a far cry from her normal attire, but she looked amazing in something other than her standard gray suit. "Wow, don't you look fancy."

"I was on a date," she said with a frown.

"I'm so sorry. You didn't have to come right away," I said.

"Are you kidding? Your call was an answer to my prayers. I never dreamed how boring a handsome man could be. I was ready to gnaw my foot off to get out of there."

"Luckily you didn't have to do that," Moose said as he smiled at Renee. "And let me echo my granddaughter's earlier comment. All I can say is wow."

She smiled at his compliment, and I saw Moose grin himself. I loved my grandfather dearly, but if Greg tried something like that, he would have lived to regret it. I didn't know how Martha put up with him, but I was happy that she did. "Thanks," Renee said. "It's nice to be appreciated."

"If I were thirty years younger and single, I can tell you one thing; you'd have your hands full," Moose said.

"Wishes and dreams," she said with a hint of laughter in her voice. "Now, let's get to work. I'm itching to get my hands on some spreadsheets and bank statements."

"You really know how to live it up, don't you?" I asked her with a smile.

"What can I say? I love it, and the more complex the puzzle, the happier I am."

"Then you're in luck," Moose said. "Evidently this estate is a real maze."

"Mazes are meant to be solved," she said.

"Then let's go," I answered.

"Jeffrey, this is Renee. Renee, I'd like you to meet Jeffrey Graham."

"I'm pleased to meet you," Jeffrey said as he extended his hand in the hallway outside the library. I wasn't all that surprised to see him light up the moment he saw her.

Renee took his hand, but then she jerked it away quickly. "You shocked me."

"Sorry. There must be a lot of static electricity in the air tonight."

"Or something," I said softly.

"What did you say, Victoria?" Renee asked me.

"Nothing. I was just mumbling to myself," I replied.

"Shall we get started?" Jeffrey asked. "I'd be happy to give you an overview of the accounts tonight, and we can get started in earnest in the morning."

Crane walked out into the hall and joined us. "Hello, all."

"Hi," I said. "Crane, meet Renee. Renee, this is Crane."

"It's nice to meet you," Crane said, "but honestly, I'm afraid you've been dragged out here at night for no reason. Everything is simple enough, and I'm certain that Jeffrey will see that once I've explained how this works to him."

"I don't mind," Renee said, and I noticed that her smile diminished a little. "If it gets too difficult to follow, you can explain it to both of us."

"I'm sorry, but what are your qualifications? Do you have any experience, or are you just here as Jeffrey's girlfriend?"

They both denied that status immediately, which was a bit funny. "Actually, I'm a CPA with a background in forensic accounting, Mr. Crane. I trust that meets with your approval."

He looked surprised by her credentials. "Of course. That would be fine."

"Let's get started then, shall we?" she asked.

"By all means," Crane said as he walked back into the other room with Renee close on his heels.

Jeffrey lingered a moment before joining them. "You know what? I like her," he said.

"I thought you might. She's quite lovely, isn't she?" I asked him.

"I meant…yes, of course…as an accountant."

Moose laughed as he patted Jeffrey's shoulder. "We know *exactly* what you mean. There's a girl in the kitchen named Margo who seems to want to talk to us, but Cassidy wasn't all that accommodating."

"He wouldn't be," Jeffrey said. "Did he try to chase you out with a meat cleaver?"

"At first, but my grandfather disarmed him," I said.

"Literally, or figuratively?" Jeffrey asked with a smile.

"Figuratively," I said.

"I could have taken it away from him if I'd wanted to," Moose said. Though he was in his seventies, my grandfather still had the mistaken impression that he was eighteen years old. Then again, so did my husband, Greg, though he was equally mistaken.

"Sure you could have," I said, and then I turned back to Jeffrey. "How do we get her alone so that we can talk to her?"

Jeffrey looked at his watch. "If you hurry, you should be able to catch Margo in the back parking area. She drives a Toyota Yaris, a red one."

"Thanks," I said.

"How exactly do we get there?" Moose asked.

"Go down this hall, take the second door from the end, and exit that way. It's a great shortcut."

"I'll have to remember that," Moose said.

"I'd better get in there," Jeffrey said. "I don't want to miss any of the fireworks."

"Do you think that there will be any?" I asked.

"I'll be disappointed in your accountant if there aren't."

"She's *yours* now," Moose said. "Accountant, I mean," he added with a grin.

Jeffrey didn't comment on that, but I could see his cheeks redden a little. It appeared that he was smitten with Renee, and who could blame him?

"Let's go," Moose said after Jeffrey was gone. "We need to catch Margo before she gets away."

"I didn't know that she was running," I said.

"You know what I mean," Moose answered.

"I do, indeed," I said.

She wasn't gone, though it was clear that she'd been dismissed before we arrived in the parking lot for the help. Margo, a tall curvy brunette with big brown eyes, was waiting for someone as she leaned against her car. I had to wonder if it was us, or perhaps a young man on staff as well.

"You're Margo, right?" I asked as Moose and I approached.

She quit leaning and took a step toward us. "That's right. May I help you with something, ma'am?"

"Are you off the clock?" I asked her.

"I am, but if I can be of assistance, I'd be glad to help."

"You can start by calling me Victoria. He's Moose. I'm pleased to meet you. I'm a server too, though *I* only work at a diner." I wanted her to trust me, but there was more to it than that. I knew what it was like to be invisible to people, and I was pretty certain that Margo didn't like the feeling any more than I did. Some folks just *refused* to see those helping them.

"Nice to meet you. I've been to The Charming Moose, but I'm sure you don't remember me."

"I'm sorry, but we get a lot of customers in the course of a day."

"Don't apologize," Margo said. "Besides, I was a blonde back then."

"I can't even picture it," Moose said. "You're a perfect brunette."

"It was a phase I was going through," she said. "I went back to this after six months."

"Margo, I noticed that you looked as though you wanted to say something in the kitchen a little bit ago. Was I right?" I asked her.

She shrugged and shuffled her feet a little. "I should keep my mouth shut; I know that."

"If you're worried about us telling anyone, you don't have to," Moose said with a gentle grin. He was everyone's grandfather at that moment, calm and safe and nurturing. I had no idea how he'd done it, but he had worked his magic just the same.

"I trust you both," she said, "though I don't have any solid reason for it. You seem so genuine. Maybe it's because I've been around so many imitations of people lately that it's refreshing to find people who are sincere."

"I've always said that once you learn how to fake sincerity, everything else is downhill from there," I said with a grin.

She laughed with me. "I know better. Still, I would hate for anyone to find out that I was speaking with the two of you."

"We could meet somewhere else if that would make you more comfortable," I said. "I'm not sure where, though, since we're tied down here for the next few days, but we can make it happen."

"I'm being silly," she said. "We can talk right here. I don't have long, though. My boyfriend is waiting for me."

"If he has any sense at all, he'll wait all night," Moose said. Coming from another older man it could have easily been construed as being a bit creepy, but my grandfather spoke with such open admiration that it was easy for Margo to take the compliment for what it was.

"He does, and he will," Margo said with a smile. It faded quickly as she added, "It's about Charlotte and Jeffrey, actually. I overheard something a few days ago that still disturbs me, especially given what happened to Mr. Trane."

"You didn't call him Curtis?" Moose asked.

"Never. He enjoyed my respect for the very reason that he never demanded it. I can't say that for any of the rest of them, including *her*."

"What were they fighting about?" I asked. "Jeffrey doesn't seem the type to argue with his employer's sister."

"No, you misunderstood me. There were two different incidents, one with Charlotte, and the other one with Jeffrey."

"Let's take Charlotte first," Moose said. "What did you overhear?"

"Evidently Mr. Trane had decided that he'd had enough, and he was changing his will and leaving North Carolina. He has land in Canada, so he was going up there to spend the time he had left in peace and quiet."

"And she didn't want him to go?" I asked.

"If he'd signed his money over to her, I don't think she would have cared if he'd gone to the moon," Margo said. "He wasn't going to do that, though."

"Where *was* his money going?" Moose asked.

"You'll have to ask his attorneys about that. All I know is they were both really angry with each other. It made me concerned for Mr. Trane's health, so I made an excuse to go in so they'd stop. Charlotte was furious with me, and she tried to fire me on the spot. Mr. Trane wouldn't hear of it, but I've got a feeling I won't be here long now that she's running things."

"I understood that *Jeffrey* was in charge of the estate," Moose said.

"He is, at least for the next few days. After that, I'm sure that I'll be let go. That's why I'm not all that worried talking to you two right now."

"What were you going to say about Jeffrey?" I asked. "Do you two have a problem?" He hadn't shown any particular interest or animosity in Margo when we'd spoken about her earlier.

"No, as far as *he* knows, we're fine."

"But not as far as *you're* concerned?" I asked softly.

"I hate thinking about it, but I'm worried that he might have had something to do with what happened to Mr. Trane."

I couldn't believe that anyone would suspect Jeffrey of murdering his boss. "What makes you say that, Margo?"

"Jeffrey owes a bad man money that he can't pay, or at least he couldn't until he became Mr. Trane's executor. There's a rumor among the staff that he'll be getting a huge payoff for doing the job, more than enough to pay off his debts."

"I can't believe that," I said. "What about you, Moose?"

"I've seen it happen to better men than him," my grandfather admitted.

"That's not all, though," Margo said. "I've been thinking about it, and it just makes sense, doesn't it?"

"What do you mean?" I asked.

"He was already at the diner when it happened. Couldn't he have put on a jacket with a hood, slipped inside the diner and killed Mr. Trane, and still make it back out to the car before you knew what happened? I know it's probably just my overactive imagination, but I love mystery shows on television, and more times than not I solve the case before the detectives do. Jeffrey had money for the motive, the means anyone could pick up, and the opportunity of being right there. How can anyone *not* consider him a suspect?"

Blast it, she made some excellent points. It hadn't even occurred to me that Jeffrey had to be a suspect, but to be fair, I hadn't known about his debts, either. Would he *really* kill Curtis Trane to pay them off, though? "Why didn't he just ask Mr. Trane for the money?" I asked her. "That would have been a great deal easier than killing him."

"Mr. Trane *hated* gambling," she said. "He never would have loaned him a dime for that, and I'm certain that Jeffrey knew that as well. It's going to keep me awake tonight, I can tell you that."

"Thanks for sharing it with us," I said.

"And you won't tell anyone what I said?" Margo asked.

"Not a soul," Moose said. "You can trust us."

She breathed out a huge sigh of relief. "Thanks for that." Margo glanced at her watch. "I've got to run. There's no reason to keep Kevin waiting any longer than I have to. Why risk it, right?"

After Margo drove off, I turned to Moose and asked, "Did you think about Jeffrey being a suspect?"

"I hate to admit it, but I didn't," my grandfather said. "Margo made a lot of sense just then though, didn't she?"

"More than I like. We need to do a little digging into Jeffrey's life."

"Great," Moose said. "Is there *anyone* here that we can trust?"

"You, me, and Renee," I said.

"That leaves a great many folks still on the hook, doesn't it?" my grandfather asked as we slowly walked back toward the house.

"Then we'd better get busy, hadn't we?"

Chapter 9

"May I help you?" Humphries asked as my grandfather and I walked back inside the mansion.

"No, we're doing just fine," Moose said.

"I was just wondering what you might have been looking for outside."

Had he been *watching* us? I wasn't about to tell him that we'd been talking to Margo, one of the place's employees. "It was a nice evening, so my grandfather and I decided to take a walk," I said. As I did, a clap of lightning hit close by, followed quickly by a loud boom of thunder.

"Before the storm hit," Moose added with a grin.

The rain came suddenly, with real purpose, pounding down with ferocity.

"It appears that you got back just in time," Humphries said.

There was another slap of lightning, and the lights all died instantly inside the mansion.

"Give it a moment," Humphries said, his voice calm despite the fact that we'd all been plunged into darkness. "This happens quite often in a storm. Nine times out of ten, the lights are back on within five seconds."

I counted to five under my breath, and then I said, "Looks like this is that tenth time. Do you have any flashlights in this place?"

"Mr. Trane preferred candles," Humphries said as he pulled out a lighter and struck it. "If you'll follow me, I'll get you both set up with candles."

I reached out and took my grandfather's hand. "This isn't *too* creepy, is it?" I asked him softly.

"If I hear somebody scream, I'm screaming, too," he answered. I couldn't *see* his smile, but I could hear it in his voice.

Humphries walked over to a sideboard and opened one of the drawers. After pulling out a single candle, he lit it with his lighter, and then closed the drawer back up. The candle gave off a soft glowing light in the darkness, and while I couldn't read by it, it was certainly bright enough to see by. I'd noticed a few candles in their stands earlier, but I'd thought of them more as props than actual tools folks used to get around the house. Humphries lit two single candles, each with its own holder, and handled one to Moose and the other to me. "Try not let them go out," Humphries said.

"We'll do our best," Moose said as he cupped his hand around the front of the flame. "Shouldn't somebody be looking for a circuit breaker?"

"I'm afraid it's not that simple," Humphries said. "The power company claims that the problem is within the home, but Mr. Trane always believed otherwise."

"The lights are out," Cassidy, the chef, called out as he came out of the kitchen holding a grand candle stand with four lit candles mounted in it.

"We noticed," Moose said.

"I'm not working in the dark," the chef said as he walked past us. "We'll finish cleaning up in the morning. I told my staff that they could leave, and I'm going to my quarters."

"That's not acceptable," Humphries said. "The evening's tasks must be completed first."

Cassidy wasn't in the mood to be argued with, whether due to recent events or the fact that we were all living by candlelight at the moment. "If you want to wash all of those dishes by hand, you're welcome to it. No power means that the dishwasher is down. Besides, I wasn't asking you for permission, I was telling you what I was doing as a courtesy. If you don't like it, have someone fire me if you can figure out who has that kind of power around here these days. Otherwise, I'd advise you to stay out of my way."

Humphries didn't comment, and as Cassidy started to walk away, I heard him say clearly, "That's what I thought," before he left.

"My apologies," Humphries said to us after the chef was gone.

"There's no need to apologize," I said. "I take it that he used to be under you?"

"As the head butler, yes, I'm in charge of the house, but with Mr. Trane's unfortunate demise, that's all open to interpretation now." He paused, and then the butler added, "Cassidy and I have been clashing for years. His open mutiny really doesn't come as a surprise to me."

A moment later, the rest of the kitchen staff left as well. There were no words exchanged, but I noticed that a few of the employees wouldn't make contact with the head butler on their way out.

There was no time, or need, to comment on it though, as Jeffrey, Renee, and Crane joined us. Evidently one of the men had been prepared for the power outage, because they were all carrying lit candles of their own.

"That's some storm raging out there," Jeffrey said as another flash of lightning illuminated the interior, blinding me for a few moments before it vanished. The crack of thunder that followed made talking impossible. That was a close one. If there had been any chance of getting power back before, that strike might have eliminated it altogether.

"I'd better go home while I still can," Renee said.

"You're more than welcome to stay the night with us," Jeffrey said. "There's plenty of room, and this weather isn't fit to drive in."

"Thanks, but I have a Land Rover with me. I've been kind of wanting to drive it in a big storm, so here's my chance." Her grin was unmistakable. "I don't think we'll get any more work done tonight, anyway. I'll see you all bright and early in the morning."

As she started to go, Jeffrey said, "I'll at least walk you to your car."

As they walked away, their candles bobbing in the darkness, I glanced at Crane and saw a look of disgust on his face.

"Is there a problem?" I asked him.

"What?" He looked surprised to be caught, because the business manager quickly buried his scowl. "No. I just hate storms, that's all. I'm going to do what Tristan and Sarah decided to do and call it a night. Humphries, show them to their rooms."

Maybe Crane just resented Jeffrey taking charge and he wanted to order someone around himself, but I wasn't ready for bed yet, and I knew that my grandfather wasn't, either. "We're going to stay down here for now."

"Suit yourself," he said, and then he walked down the hall toward the grand staircase.

"Is he *always* so pleasant?" I asked Humphries.

"The man just lost his best friend today," the butler said, surprising me with his empathy. "I'm inclined to cut him a little slack. Plus, it can't be easy for him knowing that Mr. Trane trusted his chauffeur more than him to be the estate's executor."

I hadn't had time to think about it, but that *was* odd. "Why do you think he did it?" I asked him.

"Over the past few months, Mr. Trane trusted Jeffrey with more and more things. He considered him a disinterested party, I think."

"Is he, though?" Moose asked.

"What do you mean?"

"Unless I miss my guess, he's going to be getting a pretty hefty fee for this job," Moose explained.

"I suppose so," Humphries said. There was no judgment in his voice, but I could see that the thought intrigued him as much as it had Margo. "Do you need help getting to your rooms?"

"No, I think we'll hang around and wait on Jeffrey," Moose said, and then he turned to me. "Does that suit you, Victoria?"

"I'm on board," I said.

"That was one of Mr. Trane's favorite expressions," Humphries said with a soft smile. "He loved any wordplay that involved trains."

"Why wouldn't he?" I asked. "You miss him too, don't you?"

"He gave me a second chance when no one else would," Humphries said softly. "Why wouldn't I?"

"A second chance? At what?" Moose asked him.

"At everything," Humphries said cryptically.

Before I could ask him what he meant, Jeffrey came back, wet and grinning broadly. "She wasn't kidding. That thing looked like it could climb a tree."

"If you'll excuse me, I need to make my evening rounds," Humphries said, and then he was gone before any of us even had a chance to comment.

"Don't pay any attention to him," Jeffrey said as he wiped his hands through his hair a few times. "Hump always *has* been an odd bird."

"He just told us that Mr. Trane gave him a second chance at life," I said. "Do you know anything about what he was talking about?"

"He told you that, huh? He must trust you, because it's not a story that he cares to discuss much. Hump spent a little time in prison before he joined us here."

"Prison?" I asked. "What did he do?"

"Take it easy, he didn't kill anybody," Jeffrey said. "When his last employer died, some things went missing, and the police found them in his suitcase. He swears to this day that he was set up, but he did some time for it. Curtis believed him, though, and he hired him when no one else would. The man would have taken a bullet for Curtis. For that matter, I would have myself. He had a tendency to inspire loyalty in those he felt deserved it."

"What did he inspire in those that he didn't?" Moose asked. I loved my grandfather, but sometimes I wished that he'd let the filter between his brain and his mouth have a little more input before he spoke.

"Fear, mostly," Jeffrey said. "He was a good-natured man, but I pity anyone who tried to take advantage of him."

"Like asking him to pay off their gambling debts?" I asked.

Suddenly everything got quiet.

I could see out of the corner of my eye that Moose was staring openly at me, but I was watching Jeffrey with all of my attention.

"So, you know," he said, his voice filled with quiet resignation. "I don't know why I'm all that surprised. The staff here gossips more than any hen party ever did. As far as I know, Curtis never knew about my difficulties. It gives me a little comfort knowing that now."

"Do you want to tell us about it?" I asked softly.

"Why not? The truth can't be as bad as what your imagination must be providing. I got into a poker game one night last month when I'd had too much to drink. I bet more than I had, and I lost. It's not that complicated, or sinister, either."

"Who do you owe money to?" Moose asked.

"I'm not going to get into any more details than that. I was in a jam, but I got myself out of it."

"How do you manage that?" I asked, remembering the story of Humphries and his own brush with the law.

"Did I steal it from Curtis? Is that what you're asking? The thought never crossed my mind. I pawned my grandmother's jewelry at a pawnshop in Hickory, and one of the other staffers here caught me doing it. That's when the rumors started flying around the manor."

I was certain that we'd be able to verify the chauffeur's story, but I didn't think it would matter all that much one way or the other. It appeared that we were just going to have to take Jeffrey's word that he'd paid off his debts in full, at least until we had reason to believe otherwise. I wasn't ready to take his name off of our list of suspects quite yet, though. Even if *everything* he'd just told us had been true, that just proved that he was in dire straits for money at one time. If he felt as though he couldn't ask Curtis for it, then maybe he'd arranged to get a bump in salary by becoming the estate's executor so he could redeem his pawn ticket and get everything back.

"Man, I'm beat. I'm going to go to bed if you two don't need me," he said. "I'll see you in the morning." There was another crack of lightning, and he added, "Good luck sleeping tonight."

"Are you going over to your apartment in this kind of weather?" I asked him as the thunder rumbled loudly.

"No, I'm staying here at the main house for the next few days. I would *rather* go back to my little room, but I've been instructed otherwise."

"I thought *you* were in charge of everything happening right now," Moose said.

"Do you honestly think that you two were the *only* ones who got a letter?" he asked my grandfather with a grin. "Believe me, *none* of this is my idea."

As the chauffeur started to walk away, I asked, "Who else got letters, Jeffrey?"

"Sorry, but I can't tell you that," he said, and then he walked up the stairs, his candle bobbing with each footstep.

"What do you make of that?" I asked Moose once Jeffrey was gone.

"Which part? We've been discovering so much tonight that my head's spinning. I have no idea how we're going to proceed from here, do you?"

"I have one thought," I said.

"Then let's have it, because if you don't have anything good, I'm going to bed myself."

"Go on. I can handle this on my own," I said with a grin.

"I won't even dignify that with a response," Moose said. "Wherever we're going, I'm right behind you."

"It's upstairs," I said as I started to mount the steps with my grandfather close behind me.

"Can you give me any more details than a general direction?" Moose asked me softly.

"We're going to Curtis's room to see if we can find any clues about who might have wanted to see the man dead. Do you approve of that?"

"You bet I do. That sounds like the best idea either one of us has had since we got here. Is it me, or do we seem to be reacting to our suspects' actions instead of acting on our own searching for the killer?"

"It's not just you. I know that we have to do a little bit of both, but I want to dig now."

"I'm right behind you," my grandfather said. "There's only one problem, though."

"Just one? We're in better shape than I thought, then. What problem are you talking about?"

"Which room belonged to Curtis?" he asked me.

Chapter 10

"That's a good question," I said. "To tell you the truth, I never really thought about it."

"Well, you'd better figure something out before we go barging in on our suspects, because the odds are good that we're not going to be able to find it on our own without a map," my grandfather whispered back.

"Why are you two whispering?" another voice asked out of the darkness ahead of us.

"Jeffrey, is that you?" I asked, trying my best to peer into the gloom.

"Of course it is," he said as he lit a match and then touched it back to his candle. "Who else were you expecting?"

I didn't even want to think about answering that question. "We need to snoop a little before we go to bed. Which room belonged to Curtis?" I asked.

"I'm not so sure that I like that idea much," Jeffrey said, the reluctance obvious in his voice.

"Do you think that it sounds like a party to us?" I asked. "We wouldn't do it if we didn't think that it was necessary."

"Curtis *asked* us to do this, remember?" Moose added. "Are you really all that comfortable going against his wishes?"

"No, not when you put it that way," Jeffrey said. "Come on. I'll show you the way."

"Can't you just direct us?" I asked. "I don't want anyone to think that you're cooperating with us."

"Don't worry about me," he said. "No one in this house could have a lower opinion of me than they already do. It's over here."

Jeffrey walked to the end of the hall, and as we followed, I was glad that he'd still been lingering outside his room.

Moose and I would have never found Curtis's room without him, but that did beg one question: Why hadn't he gone straight into his room instead of lurking near the top of the stairs? Had he been waiting to see what we would do next? I thought about asking him about it, but in the end, I decided to keep the question to myself. I had enough to worry about without alienating our one true ally in the house.

If Moose and I were going to solve Curtis's murder, we were going to need all of the help that we could get.

When we caught up with the chauffeur, his hand was already on the doorknob.

I put mine on his before he could open it, though. "Are you *sure* you want to go in with us?"

"I need to do this, for my sake," Jeffrey said. His voice quivered a little as he spoke. Moose silently reached out a hand and touched the chauffeur's shoulder lightly, but no words were spoken. After a few moments, my grandfather pulled his hand away, and I did the same with mine. Jeffrey took a deep breath, then he let it out slowly before he opened the door.

I nearly dropped my candle once the door was open all of the way.

Someone else was already there, a fact made obvious by the burning candle sitting alone on top of the desk near the bed.

Chapter 11

I couldn't believe it when I saw who was kneeling at the foot of the desk in Curtis's room, but I wasn't the first one to speak.

"Charlotte, what are you doing in here?" Jeffrey asked her.

"I was looking for a book I loaned Curtis a few days ago," she said as she stood.

"On the *floor*?" I asked.

"I thought it might have slipped down behind the desk," she said. "I can't find it anywhere."

"It's an odd time to be reading given the fact that we don't have any electricity, wouldn't you say?" Moose asked her.

"I can't sleep," she said simply, "and candlelight works just fine. Need I remind you that I lost my brother today?"

"What's the title of your book? We'll help you look," I answered.

"It doesn't matter," she said. "I'm certain that I would find it hopeless trying to concentrate. May I ask you three what *you* are doing here?"

She could ask, but I'm afraid that we didn't have a very good answer for her. Then Jeffrey spoke up and saved the day. "I need his checkbook ledger so I can work at settling his accounts, and Moose and Victoria volunteered to help me search," he said. "I was told that he kept it in the drawer of his desk. You haven't seen it, have you?"

"Of course not. As I said, I was looking for a book. Am I to understand that it's going to take all three of you to find it?"

Moose shrugged. "You're more than welcome to join us if you'd like."

"Thank you, but no, I don't believe so. I'll leave you to it, then. Good night."

"Good night," I said, and Moose nodded his own farewell.

Before Charlotte could leave though, Jeffrey asked, "I hate to ask this, but if you would, I'd appreciate if you'd come to me before you go into Curtis's room again. I have to inventory everything before we're ready to finalize anything."

"Of course," she said, and then Charlotte left in a huff.

After the door closed behind her, I asked him, "What that really necessary?"

"What, that last little jab at her? She's made it perfectly clear what she thinks of Curtis's choice of executors. Maybe I shouldn't have said anything, but do you honestly think she's going to give me a letter of recommendation when I leave here? I'll tell you one thing; there is no book. She was up here snooping, plain and simple."

"Isn't that what we're doing?" Moose asked him with a grin.

"Of course we are," Jeffrey said, "but at least we have some official standing here."

"You do, at any rate," I said.

"Then consider yourself deputized," Jeffrey said. "I want to find who killed Curtis more than you do. He might have asked you both to do it, but I consider it my personal duty to see this through, no matter what the consequences might be."

"What kind of consequences are you worried about?" I asked.

"I won't know that until I learn exactly what they turn out to be," he said. "Now, where should we start looking?"

"This isn't going to be easy to do by candlelight," Moose said. "I keep worrying that I'm going to set the place on fire."

"Then be extra careful," I told him. "We don't have a lot of time, so I suggest that we get busy hunting for clues."

"I think his checkbook might be a good place to start at that," Jeffrey said. "I'll take the desk, Moose gets the closet, and Victoria gets the dresser. Hang on a second." He walked to the closet and pulled out a medium-sized box that would have held two standard loaves of bread. "Anything that looks interesting can go in here, and we can sort it out later."

I wasn't sure that I was all that crazy about his plan. If we did as Jeffrey suggested, we'd be putting all of our clues into his hands. If he was telling the truth when he said that he wanted to find Curtis's killer, we wouldn't have a problem, but if he wanted everything so he could destroy anything that might make him look culpable, we would be playing into his hands.

"Tell you what," I said, "I'll agree to that, as long as Moose and I get custody of the box."

I saw Jeffrey face me, and in the flickering glow of his candlelight, he looked a little ominous to me. "What's the matter, Victoria? Don't you trust me?"

"Do you want the truth? I don't trust *anybody* in this house tonight," I said.

"Hey, I resent that," Moose said.

"Would it be better if I said anyone in close contact with Curtis?"

"I can live with that," Moose said. He turned to Jeffrey and he asked, "What do you say to Victoria's proposal? Can you live with my granddaughter's plan?"

"I don't particularly care for being dumped in with the rest of them, but I can see your point. Okay. You can have first crack at whatever you find, but when you're done with it, you need to turn it all over to me. I wasn't kidding when I told Charlotte that I'd have to do a full inventory of Curtis's possessions."

"Agreed," I said. "Let's get started, shall we?"

It took forty minutes for the three of us to search Curtis's room by candlelight. We had a decent assortment of things in the box now, but there was nothing earth-shattering in any of our finds. I'd found some old letters, Jeffrey had found something that looked suspiciously like a diary besides the checkbook and ledger he'd discovered, and Moose had found four notebooks that sported the oddest collection of expressions that I'd ever seen.

"What exactly are these?" I asked Jeffrey as I held one up to my light.

"Curtis called them his musings," Jeffrey said. "After he first got sick, he started recording his thoughts in there. I might publish them myself some day as a tribute to him."

"I'll make sure that you get these back when Moose and I are finished with them," I said.

"I'd appreciate that. Now, I just need this," Jeffrey said as he reached into the box of collected treasures and tried to grab the checkbook.

"Hold on a second. You agreed to let us have *everything*," I said, grabbing it before he could. "No exceptions."

"Victoria, I need those checks," Jeffrey protested.

"Go ahead. Give him the checks," Moose said.

Was my grandfather actually going to go along with this? "I don't think that it's a good idea. There might be entries in it that lead us to Curtis's killer."

"I agree. I didn't say a word about giving him the ledger, but there is no earthly reason *not* to give him the checks."

I could see the logic of that, so I pulled out the checks and handed the sheaf to Jeffrey. "There you go. You don't mind if I keep the ledger, do you?"

"For now," he said as he tucked the checks into his pocket. As he scanned the room, Jeffrey asked, "Is there anything that we've missed?"

"I don't suppose there's any real way of knowing that," I said. I looked around again myself, but I didn't see anything that looked the least bit pertinent to our investigation. "Moose, would you like to go over what we've found in my room?"

I looked over at my grandfather in the flickering light from my candle, and I realized that he looked tired. That's why it didn't really surprise me when he suggested, "That sounds good to me, but let's wait until morning, okay? It's been a long day, and I'm beat."

"That sounds like a plan," I said

As we walked out of Curtis's room, I was surprised to find that we were greeted by Sarah, Tristan, and Crane, all standing together with their candles flickering from the breeze we'd just created opening the door.

"What exactly have you three been doing in there?" Crane asked.

"Yes, Uncle Curtis didn't like anyone to go in his room," Sarah added.

"If you get to look around in there, then we should, too," Tristan said as he spied the box I had tucked under one arm. It was a little awkward holding the candle as well, but I managed it without setting the drapes on fire. "What's in there?" he demanded.

"Just some paperwork and things that might come in handy while we're trying to settle the estate," Jeffrey said.

"Let us see what you've got," Crane insisted as he reached for the box.

I wasn't about to let him have it though, and neither was Moose. My grandfather stepped between us. "This isn't open for debate, folks. We're not in a democracy at the moment. There's only one person in charge, and that's Jeffrey Graham."

The chauffeur looked uncomfortable having everyone on the landing staring at him. After a moment, he said, "Believe me when I tell you that I'm not trying to make anyone's life uncomfortable. Let me do the job that Curtis asked me to do, and then I'll be out of your hair forever."

Tristan shrugged. "That sounds reasonable enough. I can live with that."

Jeffrey looked at Sarah. "What about you?"

She glanced at her brother, who shrugged slightly. "Whatever Tristan says is fine with me."

Jeffrey saved the business manager for last. "What do you say, Crane? It's pretty clear that you think I'm in over my head, and you might be right, but I'm going to see this through, with your help or without it. That being said, I'd much rather have your support if I can."

"I've been cooperative so far, haven't I?" Crane asked.

"I suppose so," Jeffrey said as he nodded.

"Then there's no reason to believe that I'll act otherwise in the future. As you say, Curtis had his reasons for doing what he did, and I plan to respect them, no matter what my personal opinion might be about the decisions that he made." Wow, that was a pretty clear shot at Jeffrey, but he didn't react to it.

"Excellent," the chauffeur said. "Now, if you'll all excuse me, I'm heading off to bed. Tomorrow is going to be another brutal day, I'm afraid."

As we split up, Sarah asked petulantly, "What's Victoria doing with the box? I thought that *you* were in charge of it, Jeffrey."

"I am," he replied, "but it's late, and I'm tired. We'll go over it in the morning, but for tonight, it will remain in Victoria's possession, per Curtis's instructions." Technically it was even true, since Moose and I were going to try to use the contents of the box to help solve his murder.

"I wouldn't mind seeing that particular letter myself," Crane said softly.

"I would never dream of showing it to you," I said with a smile. "Nor would I ask to see yours, if you got one. They are personal in nature; that's my interpretation of mine, at any rate. Good night all."

"Good night," they said in an uneven chorus in return.

"Guard your discoveries well," Jeffrey said as I started to close the door to my room.

"Do you think someone might try to steal them?" I asked, suddenly feeling a whole new level of paranoia.

"No, not out from under your nose," Jeffrey said. "On second thought, maybe I should keep them for you myself."

I wasn't happy with the prospect of someone trying to get into my room to see what we'd found, but neither did I care for the idea that Jeffrey would be watching over them. "I'll be careful."

"That's all that I can ask," he said.

Once I had the large solid oak door closed and locked, I took the chair from a nearby desk and jammed it under the doorknob. Nobody was getting into my room tonight. As an extra precaution, I removed the contents of the box and stuffed everything into one of the pillowcases on the bed. As a substitute, I stuck a few paperback novels in their place that I'd brought along just in case I'd have time to read. There wasn't much worry about that happening. The books gave the box a nice heft, and I put it prominently on the desk near my bed.

I had one more thing I wanted to do before I turned in for the night. I pulled out my cellphone and dialed Greg using my speed dial. I might not be able to kiss my husband goodnight, but at least I'd get the opportunity to chat with him for a few minutes before I went to sleep.

"I didn't wake you, did I?" I asked Greg as he answered the phone on the seventh ring.

"No, I was just watching a little television," he said, and then I heard him stifle a yawn. I had a hunch that he'd nodded off, but I wasn't about to say anything about it. "You've had yourself a big day, haven't you, Victoria? How are the accommodations there?"

"Do you remember that creepy old hotel we stayed in when we went to the beach the year we got married?" I asked him.

"Are you talking about the one with the unpainted cinderblock walls and that nasty tub that we were both afraid to try?" he asked.

"That's the one."

There was a moment's pause, and then Greg asked me, "Really? Is it that bad?"

"On the contrary. Imagine the opposite of that, and *that's* what this place is like," I said as I laughed. As I looked around the room, I began to describe it to him. "Here goes. Picture dark hardwood floors that look to be a hundred years old and polished to a sheen, wainscoting surrounding the entire room, which happens to be bigger than our living room and dining room combined by the way, crown moldings, art on the walls suitable for any high-end gallery, a bed fit for royalty, and a beautiful bathroom with everything I could ever want."

"Wow, it sounds like you're really roughing it," he said. "Take some pictures with your phone so I can see them when you get home."

"I will," I said. "How was the diner today without me?"

"Well, it was touch and go for a while there, but we managed to pull through."

"How did Stephanie do?"

Greg sighed. "Well, she's not you, but she managed okay."

Was it evil of me to be happy with that report? I decided to give myself a break. After all, who wanted to be replaced so easily at what they did? "Don't worry. I'm sure that she'll be fine," I said.

"Probably, but you're a tough act to follow. How's the investigation going?"

"It's confusing, but I'm not all that surprised by it at this point. You know as well as I do that it takes some time to gather all of the facts."

"Has Sheriff Croft been by yet?"

"No," I said. "Why do you ask?"

"He was at the diner just before we closed. I have a feeling that you're going to be seeing him tomorrow. He made it a point to ask me if I'd heard from you, by the way."

"Was he looking for help?" I asked with a laugh.

"He wasn't in a great mood, so I'm guessing that it's not going too well for him on his end."

"He's in good company," I said.

"Would it help any if you ran down your suspects?" Greg asked.

"Probably, but I doubt that I could get them all to stand still in the parking lot that long."

He laughed. "Victoria, has anyone told you that you have a warped sense of humor?"

"Do you mean besides you?" I asked. It was so good speaking with my husband. I tried never to take it for granted that we worked together, but it really hit home when we were separated.

"I do," he said.

"Then yes, a time or two. Are you sure you wouldn't mind being my sounding board?"

"Hey, that's why I'm here," Greg said.

"Okay, here goes. We have a niece and nephew, a brother and sister named Sarah Harper and Tristan Wellborne. Sarah's spoiled rotten, and Tristan is a wannabe artist who thinks he's Picasso's natural successor. After that, there's Curtis's sister, an imposing old gal named Charlotte who won't tolerate being second-guessed about anything. Besides family, there's a man who's referred to only as Crane who was Curtis's business manager." I took a deep breath, and then I added, "And finally, we've got Jeffrey himself."

"The chauffeur made your list of suspects?" Greg asked. "How did that happen? I thought that he was one of the good guys."

"He still might be," I said, "but he gambles, and what's worse, he loses more than he wins."

"Does he stand to inherit from Curtis's estate?"

"He doesn't need to. Evidently the stipend for being the executor of the estate pays a great deal of money. I'm having a hard time believing it, but Moose thinks that it's a viable option."

"When it comes to motive, especially when greed is involved, I'd trust your grandfather's gut if I were you."

"That's why Jeffrey's still on our list. Oh, by the way, we called in Renee to help Jeffrey go over the books. I thought Crane was going to have a fit when he found out."

"If anyone can get to the bottom of those finances, it's Renee. That was a smart move to call her."

"Moose and I suggested it, but Jeffrey is the one in charge. He's not very popular around here at the moment. Nobody can figure out why Curtis gave the executer's post to Jeffrey instead of his longtime business manager and friend."

"I'm sure he had his reasons," Greg said. "Is *everyone* on your list of suspects staying there at the house with you?"

"There's plenty of room," I said. "This place is huge."

"Victoria, I hope you're being careful. You're vulnerable there; you know that, don't you? As a matter of fact, both of you are."

"We're watching each other's backs," I said. "There's nobody but you that I'd rather have keeping an eye out for me than my grandfather."

"Keep him safe," Greg said.

"That might be a little tough, but I'll do what I can," I said. "Oh yeah, the power's out here, too; did I mention that?"

"You did not," Greg answered, sounding a little alarmed. "What happened? Was it cut on purpose, do you think?"

"Nothing as ominous as all that. We had a powerful storm move through, and evidently it's not that odd to lose the electricity here. Did you get anything in town?"

"We heard a few rumbles in the distance and it rained a little, but all in all, it wasn't much to talk about."

"We must have gotten the brunt of it here," I said.

Greg paused, and then my husband said, "Double-lock your door if you can."

"It's locked, and I have a chair jammed under the knob for good measure," I said as I looked over at my makeshift dead bolt.

"Good," he said. "What's on tap for tomorrow?"

"Moose and I are going to look through the things we found when we searched Curtis's room tonight by candlelight. Jeffrey was with us, and the three of us caught Charlotte in there snooping around."

"What excuse did you give her for your digging?" he asked.

I never got a chance to tell him, though. My cellphone beeped twice, and I saw that the battery was nearly dead. "Greg, my phone's dying. I'll call you tomorrow."

"Good—" was all that I heard when it finally died completely.

I'd brought my charger with me, but a fat lot of good it was going to do. Without power, I was without a cellphone until I could charge it back up. It hadn't been all that long ago that I hadn't even had a cellphone, and I'd resisted the impulse to buy one, but now I felt vulnerable without one.

I had a hunch that I was going to be in for a long night.

To make matters worse, the storm picked up again, and as lightning flashed just outside my window, I decided that a candlelit bath would be a luxury that I didn't need. I slipped into my jammies and crawled into the big bed, preparing myself for a long and restless night.

Chapter 12

I woke up sometime in the middle of the night in complete and utter darkness, and at first I thought that the storm must have been what had brought me fully awake.

Then, as the lightning flashed outside, my room was lit up for one brief instant.

And though I couldn't see a face, I could clearly make out a figure standing just a few feet from my bed.

Chapter 13

I'm not all that proud of what happened next, but who could blame me? It wasn't easy waking up and finding somebody in my room who didn't belong there.

So I screamed.

The lightning died, and as the thunder boomed, I wondered if anyone had even heard me. I fumbled for the candle and the matchbook Humphries had given me, but the problem was that I'd been blinded by the intensity of the lightning flash. I heard a swooshing sound nearby as I knocked the candlestick over. At least it hadn't been lit, so there was no danger of me starting a fire. I slid out of the bed, found the candle, and then I groped around on the nightstand until I found the matches. As I lit one, I half expected whoever was in there to blow it out. If they had, my earlier scream would have sounded like a whisper compared to the one I was about to let loose.

The match flared for a moment, and then the flame steadied. I lit the candle, prepared for a fight.

No one was there, though.

I searched the room, including under the massive bed and behind the shower door, but I was alone. Worse yet, the chair was still jammed solidly under the bedroom doorknob.

No one had gotten in that way.

Was it possible that I'd just dreamed it?

There was a knock coming from the hallway.

"Who is it?" I asked.

"It's Moose," my grandfather said. "Victoria, are you okay?"

"Hang on a second," I said. I struggled to pull the chair out from its place, and I had a tough time moving it because I'd wedged it under the knob so tightly.

"Victoria," Moose said again more urgently as he knocked

again.

I finally managed to unlock the door and I let him in.

He had a candle of his own, and he was standing there in his pajamas and robe. "Did I hear you scream earlier?" he asked.

"Someone was in my room," I said.

"Let me have a look," Moose said urgently as he brushed past me.

At least no one else had heard my scream. I locked the door behind him, and then I said, "Moose, I've already searched the place thoroughly."

"Then it won't hurt if I have a look around myself," he said. My grandfather checked every space there that was large enough to hide someone, including the back of the closet and under the chest of drawers. After he was satisfied, he said, "Sometimes after I eat a particularly spicy meal, I've been known to have nightmares that strangers are in the house," he said.

"This was no nightmare," I told him. "I'm certain of it."

"Take it easy. I believe you. Was it a man or a woman?"

"I couldn't tell you. Whoever it was, their back was turned to me. It was eerily like what happened at the diner yesterday."

Moose frowned. "I know that you don't want to hear this, but it could still just have been a nightmare," he said. "Why *wouldn't* you have bad dreams about what happened, Victoria? Someone came into our space and killed a friend of ours. I've had a few nightmares about that tonight myself, and I wasn't even there when it happened."

"It was real enough," I said as I looked around the room again. The light from one candle wasn't all that much, but with Moose's added to the illumination, I could see decently now.

As I looked at the desk, I suddenly realized that I had proof.

The box we'd used to collect clues from Curtis's room was gone.

Chapter 14

"The box is gone, Moose," I said calmly.

He looked hard at me. "Where did you put it?"

"It was right there on top of the desk when I went to sleep," I said.

Moose shook his head. "That's really too bad. I had high hopes for what we found, and now it's all gone."

"Not so fast," I said as I reached for the pillowcase where I'd stuffed everything. I felt a little dread in the pit of my stomach as I grabbed it. How could the killer possibly know what I'd done with the actual contents? Then again, if the killer watched me hide everything through some kind of secret panel or hidden camera, we didn't have a chance.

Thankfully, it was all there.

"I've got it," I said.

Moose's grin was broad and wide. "That was brilliant, Victoria, just brilliant. What made you hide everything in a pillowcase?"

"I figured that it couldn't hurt," I said.

"I'm glad that you did. You outsmarted a murderer tonight, young lady."

"What if they come back when they find the two paperbacks I stashed in the box? There is no way that I'm getting back to sleep tonight."

"Bring everything with you. You're bunking in my room tonight. You can have the bed. I don't sleep as much as I used to, so I'll stand guard duty."

"I don't feel right putting you out like that," I protested.

"Sorry, but I'm going to have to insist. Come on, it will be fun."

I honestly wasn't all that happy about spending what was left of the night by myself, so I really didn't fight him that hard. "I'll come with you, but only if we take shifts staying awake."

"Sold, as long as I get the first watch."

"I can live with that," I said. I hesitated before I made a move to leave, though. "Moose, how did they get in?"

"Humphries told us that this place was riddled with secret passageways, remember?"

"Then what makes you think that your room is going to be any safer than this one?" I asked.

"Because we'll be ready for whoever it is the next time," he said. My grandfather sounded a lot more confident than I felt, but really, I didn't have much choice. We had to stay at the house since that's where all of our suspects were, but there was no way that I was spending another night alone. I would rather sleep a bit and then wake up in the morning a little cranky than wrestle with the killer.

"Let's go, Victoria."

"I've still got to pack my bag," I said.

"You can't do that. We don't want the killer to realize that you saw them."

"Moose, I screamed, remember? *Nobody's* going to forget that."

"Maybe not," my grandfather said, "but I'm betting they believe you'll pass it all off as a bad dream come morning. After all, what proof is there that they were even here?"

"I don't know. That stolen box is a pretty big clue," I replied.

"Yes, you're right. I hadn't thought about that. Do you have any suggestions?"

"We could always tell Jeffrey and the others that I misplaced it. We can even have them help us look for it in the morning if we decide that it's a good idea."

"That might work if we get desperate," Moose said. "I'm afraid that it's going to make you look a little scatterbrained, though."

"If that's the worst thing that happens to me in the next few days, I'll consider myself lucky," I said. "Besides, it could be helpful watching how everyone reacts to the news when I admit that I had a nightmare last night. It might make the killer complacent enough to make another mistake."

"What did they do wrong this time?" Moose asked me as we walked to his room.

"They tried to play me for a fool," I said, "and I'm not about to forget that."

I don't know how I managed it, but I slept a bit more after all. I stretched as I got out of Moose's bed, and I found him nodding off in one of the chairs.

I touched his arm lightly, and he came straight awake.

"Moose, it's morning."

"What? I must have dozed off. Did they get your pillowcase?" he asked.

I checked and found the contents intact. "We've still got everything we took from Curtis's room."

"I can't *believe* that I fell asleep. Some watchdog I turned out to be."

"Don't beat yourself up about it. Nothing happened."

"No," my grandfather said, "but it *might* have."

"Cheer up," I said. "It's a brand-new day, and we've got a lot to do."

"You're right, there's no use worrying about spilled milk under the bridge," he said with a wry smile. That's when I knew that he was going to be okay. My grandfather enjoyed wordplay, and mixing old adages was right up his alley. "What's first on our list?"

"I don't know about you," I said, "but the first thing that *I* want to do is to figure out how someone got into my room last night."

"I'm curious about that myself. You might not know this, but I've studied some of the old house plans that sported secret passageways."

I looked at him oddly. "Why in the world would you ever do that?"

He grinned at me. "I wanted to put one in the house Martha and I were building, but she wouldn't let me."

"I find it hard to believe that she'd say no about something like that." My grandmother enjoyed a good joke as much as anyone, and having a passageway in her home that no one knew about fit that bill perfectly.

"She was on board until she found out how much square footage it would have eaten," Moose said. "Still, I picked up a few tricks when I was studying."

"Then let's see what we can find," I said.

"You go on. I want to change first. You don't mind, do you?"

"Go right ahead," I said, though I wasn't really sure that I felt brave enough to go back into my room alone. At least it was morning, and with fresh light pouring in through the windows, I didn't have to deal with candlelight. "I'll see you soon."

I opened his bedroom door slightly and peeked out into the hallway. No one was up yet. Well, they might have been, but if they were, they weren't out of their rooms. I hurried down the hall to my room, and I was breathing hard as I opened it, slipped inside, and locked it behind me. As I changed quickly, I felt a little paranoid, as though someone might be watching me. That fear was not without merit. I had to admit that I felt better once I was in fresh jeans and T-shirt. Moose still wasn't there yet, so I decided to have a look around myself. As I approached a paneled wall, I started pressing everything in sight, from moldings to wall sconces to the panels themselves. While I was searching, I flipped on a table lamp to see if our power had been restored yet. It had, much to my delight, so I got out my charger and my phone and I hooked everything up.

After I plugged it in, though, there was no green light displayed on my phone showing that it was charging.

I tried another outlet, and sure enough, this time the light shone brightly. Was the first outlet dead, or was it something else entirely? Getting down on my hands and knees, I tried looking into the slots where the plug went, but I couldn't see anything that didn't look right. Glancing around the room, I couldn't find anything to use to unscrew the wall plate, but then I remembered that I had a pair of tweezers in my overnight bag. Holding them on an angle, I was able to work the compressed blades into the slot of the screw that held everything in place, and I started to turn it. It took a few tries, but I finally got it all the way out, and I pulled the plate off.

No wonder I couldn't get the phone to charge.

There were no wires leading into the outlet, but there was a single thin rod threaded through the back of it.

I pressed the outlet and realized that it was loose. I tried the top, and then the bottom, toggling it back and forth like a switch.

Nothing happened.

And then I turned back to the paneled wall where I'd been searching earlier.

One of the sections looked a little out of alignment, and as I got close to it, I could see that instead of being attached to the wall, it was on a hinge.

I'd found my secret door.

Before I could explore further, though, there was a knock at my door. Was it Moose, or had someone come to see what I was up to?

"One second," I said as I put the outlet cover back in place and replaced the screw. As I walked to the door, I took a moment to push the secret entrance closed. If it was Moose, I was sure that I could repeat the results, but if someone else was visiting, I didn't want there to be any evidence of what I'd found.

The knocking was harder now.

"Victoria, are you okay?" It was Moose.

I opened the door and let him in. "Take it easy. I'm fine."

"What took you so long?" he said as he rushed in.

"I found something," I said.

"Well, don't keep me waiting. What is it?"

"Watch this," I said as I knelt down by the outlet again. I didn't have to remove the cover this time. Pushing on the top, then the bottom, and then the top again, I grinned up at Moose as I saw the door release behind him.

He didn't see it, though. "I don't get it."

"Turn around," I said.

He saw the passageway instantly. "How did you *do* that?"

"I'd love to say that I figured it out all by myself, but I was actually just trying to charge my cellphone."

"It's not what I was expecting," my grandfather said as he peered into the darkness. Moose started to step in, but something was holding him back.

"What's wrong?" I asked him.

"You found this. You should get to explore it first."

"You don't mind?"

"It's killing me not to go first, but right is right," he said. "I'll stay here and guard your exit. Would you like to take a candle with you?"

"I guess I'd better," I said as I grabbed the one on the desk. "This is going to be so cool."

"Don't take any chances," he said as he lit the candle in my hand. "Just see where it leads and then come straight back to me."

"I will," I said.

I opened the door the rest of the way and started inside. I was glad that Moose had suggested the candle. There was very little light inside the passageway, and as I made the first turn, the light from the door was nearly gone. There was a stale smell in the air, combined with something that smelled a little industrial to me. I walked slowly, looking at the plaster and lath corridor on either side of me. There had to be another door somewhere. How else had my late-night visitor gotten in?

The passage dead-ended, though.

It appeared that I'd been visited by a ghost after all.

That was nonsense, of course. On my way back, I studied the walls a little more closely, and upon further examination, I spotted a section that didn't look like the rest. Gently putting my hand on it, I pushed lightly, and the one part of the wall swung back effortlessly.

It didn't put me directly out into another room, though. I saw an area had been chipped away, and one single beam of light came through.

It was clearly a peephole.

But what could I see when I looked through it?

Chapter 15

It was the hallway where we'd all discussed things the night before! I was all set to open the door to see how it was accessed from the other side when I heard voices.

My hand stopped, and I moved back to the spyhole.

"I don't like this one little bit," Tristan said, his voice soft enough to nearly make it impossible for me to hear him.

"You don't have to like it. You just need to fix it," his sister, Sarah, said. She was making no effort to keep her voice down.

"Do you want everyone in the house to overhear us?" Tristan asked her in a harsh whisper. "Speak softer, Sarah."

"No one's even up yet," she said with disgust, "and I wouldn't be either if you hadn't barged into my room. What was so urgent, anyway?"

"I don't trust those two," he said.

"Which two are those?" she asked him.

"Moose and Victoria, of course. Who *else* could I mean?" Tristan asked.

"I think that Jeffrey and Crane are a much bigger threat to our immediate interests than two short-order cooks," Sarah said. I'd never been a short-order cook in my life, but I had a suspicion that this wasn't the time to point it out.

"Why do you say that?"

"Because *they* control the money. If anyone's going to hurt us, it's going to be them."

Tristan shook his head. "I'm not as worried about that."

"Well, you should," Sarah said.

"Why do you say that?" Tristan asked.

She was about to answer when a third person joined them.

"Good morning," Jeffrey said as he entered the space.

"Morning," Tristan and Sarah said in unison.

"Have either one of you seen Moose and Victoria?" he

asked. “I’d like to speak with them.”

“Try their rooms,” Tristan said.

“I’ll do that.” The chauffeur started toward my room, and I knew that I had to hurry, but as I was leaving the hidden space, I heard Jeffrey say, “The three of us will talk later.”

“I imagine that we will,” Sarah said, and there was a frigid air in her voice that Jeffrey noticed immediately.

“You don’t like any part of this, do you?” he asked her.

“Which part are you talking about?” Sarah asked in turn.

“The fact that I have a hand in your future,” Jeffrey said.

“Don’t delude yourself. All that you’re *really* good for is something that any teenager with a driver’s license can do,” Sarah said. As she’d said it, she’d sounded remarkably like her aunt.

If it stung Jeffrey, he didn’t show it. Instead, he replied with a smile, “That may have been true a few days ago, but I shouldn’t have to remind you that things have a way of changing.”

Jeffrey didn’t wait for her reply, so neither could I. I hurried down the passageway so I could get back into my room before he showed up knocking on my door.

As I rushed though, I forgot to shield my candle, and it suddenly went out.

I was plunged back into darkness.

There was no way that I was going to make it back in time now.

As I felt along one wall, a light suddenly appeared before me. I felt my heart jump until I saw that it was my grandfather. “What took you so long? I thought something happened to you.”

“Turn around and go back. We have to hurry.”

He did as I asked, and soon we were back in my room. I shut the passage door behind us and started for the door when there was the expected knock.

“Act naturally,” I told Moose before I opened it.

“How did you know that someone was coming?”

"I'll tell you when Jeffrey's gone," I said.

There was another tap, and then before he could finish knocking a second time, I opened the door. "Jeffrey, we were just going to breakfast," I said, hoping that he couldn't tell that I'd been rushing to get there.

"Let me walk you down," he said. "I trust you slept well."

"I did," I lied.

Moose stretched a little. "I wasn't as fortunate. The older I get, the harder it is for me to sleep away from home."

"I appreciate your sacrifice," he said. "Shall we go?"

"Give us one second to chat, okay?" I asked.

Jeffrey looked a little puzzled by my request, but he agreed to it nonetheless.

When the door closed again, I whispered, "Where are the things we found in Curtis's room?"

"You're not the only one good at hiding things," he said. "Don't worry about it right now, Victoria. It's all taken care of."

"Is it safe?" I asked.

"I'll be shocked if anyone finds it. Now, let's go. We don't want to make anyone suspicious."

"That ship has probably sailed already," I said. I wanted to know where Moose had hidden the potential clues that we'd found, but I understood his caution in telling me.

After all, I'd just seen for myself that the walls had both eyes and ears.

"There you are," Tristan said as we walked into the dining room. "Where have you two been?"

"Tristan, don't be rude," Charlotte said.

"Sorry, but breakfast is supposed to be served on time around here."

"You could have always started without us," Moose said.

"That's against the rules of the house. No one eats until everyone is seated."

"Tristan, stop being such a nit," his sister, Sarah, said. "We can't get started until Crane gets here, as well."

Charlotte frowned, and then she turned to the butler, who was hovering nearby. "Humphries, go fetch Crane, would you? Please tell him that we're all waiting for him."

As the butler left, Sarah asked me, "So, what did you find in Curtis's room last night?"

Before I could answer, Charlotte asked, "You took something from my brother's room? By what right did you do that?"

"Don't be that way. You *know* that I was with them," Jeffrey said. "I gave them my permission. After all, they're here by Curtis's explicit request, and I was told in no uncertain terms to help them in whatever way that I could, so that's what I've been doing."

"It's still all rather unseemly," Charlotte said softly.

"So is murder," Jeffrey answered.

Wow, those two really didn't like each other.

"Victoria, you never answered my question," Sarah said.

"Honestly, we haven't had a chance to examine everything closely yet. I'm not all that comfortable saying anything until we've had a little more time to see what we've uncovered."

"Did any of you hear a woman scream last night?" Tristan asked lightly. "Or did I just dream it?"

"I'm afraid that was me," I said. It was time to go into our backstory.

"Nightmares, dear?" Charlotte asked.

"Exactly. I dreamed that someone was standing over my bed watching me sleep," I said as I sheepishly looked around the table. No one gave anything away though, at least not that I could see. Maybe Moose had better luck picking up on a subtle clue.

"I hate those," Sarah said.

"Do you get them often, sis?" Tristan asked her.

"What I dream about is none of your business, big brother," she said.

He found that amusing for some reason, but at least his low chuckle was the only answer that he gave.

Jeffrey said, "As a matter of fact, I had a few nightmares myself last night."

"It's an epidemic," Tristan said with a smile, though I didn't find anything amusing about it. I decided not tell anyone that I'd lost the box of clues just yet, because I didn't feel all that comfortable about playing the fool. What kind of idiot loses the only clues she has, anyway? Besides, if I pretended that the box hadn't been stolen in the middle of the night, maybe it would make the killer believe I was just a scatterbrained woman. Ordinarily I hated being underestimated, but if it helped me catch the murderer, I could live with that for the moment.

Humphries rushed back into the dining room. "May I have a word, Ms. Trane?"

She started to stand when Jeffrey spoke up. "If you've got something to say, everyone should hear what it is."

Charlotte loomed over him in his seat. "You may be in charge of my late brother's estate, but it gives you no power over me, do you hear me?"

Jeffrey just shrugged. "I don't see it that way, and neither do the lawyers Curtis hired to back me up. For all intents and purposes, until the last bit of paperwork is filed, *I'm* the one running things. If you'd feel more comfortable in your home, you can go there at any time. I'll see to it that you're informed about the most significant findings that we make here. What do you say? Should Humphries move your bags for you, Charlotte?"

"I'm fine right where I am," she said. After a cold stare in Jeffrey's direction, she turned back to the butler. "Go on, Humphries. Tell us all what you've discovered. Why is Crane late?"

"That's the problem, ma'am," he said. "Mr. Crane isn't in his room."

"Then he's most likely just gone for a stroll before breakfast," Sarah said shortly. "He can't be *that* hard to find. I know this place is big, but it's not *that* big."

"You don't understand," Humphries said. "It appears that

there was a struggle in his room sometime last night. I got the distinct impression that when he left, it wasn't by choice."

"Let's go take a look," Moose said as he stood and started for the staircase.

"I'm right behind you," I said as I followed him out of the dining room. "Humphries, lead the way."

"What about breakfast?" Sarah asked with a whine.

"That can wait," Charlotte answered as she joined us.

"Well, *I'm* not traipsing off looking for someone who doesn't want to be found." She appeared to settle into her seat with no plans to budge at all.

Her brother clearly had other ideas, though. Tristan pulled her arm up. "Come on, Sarah. No one gets left behind. Wouldn't you feel safer with me by your side?"

"Barely," she replied.

"I'll take what I can get," he said with a smile. "Let's all go look."

As we headed up the stairs together, Jeffrey touched my shoulder. "What do you think this is all about, Victoria?"

"I honestly don't know," I said.

"Do you think he's really gone?" Jeffrey asked.

"I don't doubt it. The question I want answered is if it was by choice, or by force."

"What a nightmare," Jeffrey said. "We've got a ton of work to do today." He glanced at his watch. "Renee is due in twenty minutes."

"Could that be why Crane's missing?" Moose asked.

"What do you mean?" Jeffrey replied.

"I'm just wondering if there was something in those ledgers that he didn't want you two to find."

Jeffrey frowned. "Curtis trusted him with his life."

"Let's just hope that it wasn't misplaced trust," I said as Humphries paused in front of a door down the hallway from where Moose and I had stayed last night.

"Go on, open it," Charlotte snapped at him.

The butler paused long enough for Jeffrey to nod his

approval before he opened the door. Smart man. He knew who was really in charge.

The room was a mess, with pillows and blankets strewn across the floor. The mattress was askew, and I noticed a few drops of blood near the bathroom from where I was standing outside. "Nobody needs to go in there," I snapped.

"Why on earth not?" Charlotte asked. "He might be hurt."

I turned to Humphries. "Did you search the room? What about the bathroom?"

The butler looked unhappy about the scrutiny. "I never dreamed that it wouldn't be acceptable. As I said, he's not here. I checked the restroom myself."

"That settles it," I said. "Lock the door right now."

"I'd do it if I were you," Jeffrey said, and the butler closed the door and locked it.

"That's not fair," Tristan said. "I didn't get a good look."

"Sorry, but until the police arrive, no one is going in there," I answered.

"Is that really necessary?" Charlotte asked in that tone of disdain she'd clearly mastered so well over the years.

"It is," I replied. "Would you like *us* to call the sheriff for you, Jeffrey, or would you rather handle it yourself?"

"Call him," he said. After another glance at his watch, he said, "I'm sorry, but I have to get something in my stomach before Renee gets here."

"Finally, someone is talking sense," Sarah said. "I'll join you."

"Anyone else?" Jeffrey asked.

"Why not?" Tristan asked. "The excitement's over for now."

Humphries started to trail Charlotte when Jeffrey stopped him. "If you don't mind, will you keep guard over this door until the police arrive? No one is to get in, and I mean no one. Do you understand?"

"Yes, sir, of course," he said as he pivoted and placed himself squarely in front of the missing business manager's room.

"Was that really necessary?" Charlotte asked him as we all walked back down the stairs.

"If I'm going to make a mistake, I'd rather err on the side of caution," he said.

"I myself think that it's a great idea," Moose said loudly. "I would have done the same thing myself."

"If you were in charge, you mean," Charlotte said.

"Ma'am, no disrespect intended, but I've rarely waited for someone else's permission in my life. Besides, it's usually better to ask for forgiveness after I've done whatever I intended to do in the first place."

"What an interesting life your wife must lead," Charlotte said.

"We still manage to have our moments," Moose said with that dashing grin of his, but I knew that he was wasting the wattage. Charlotte appeared to be one of those rare ladies who was immune to my grandfather's charm.

"What should we do now?" I asked Moose softly as we both lagged behind the crowd.

"I think breakfast is an excellent idea for *all* of us," he said.

"So that we can keep our eyes on everyone else?" I asked him.

"Well, I suppose there's that, but to be honest with you, I'm starving. I've got a hunch that I'll think a lot better on a full stomach."

"And if you don't, at least you get to eat, right?" I asked with a smile.

"That's my girl," he answered as he took out his phone. "I'm guessing that yours is still charging. Am I right?"

"It's in my room, yes," I said. "Would you like me to talk to Sheriff Croft?"

"No, I can handle it," he said. My grandfather started to dial, and then he suddenly handed the phone to me.

As I took it, I said, "I thought *you* were going to do it."

"I want to keep an eye on that crew," he said as he hurried past me.

I faded back, finished dialing the sheriff's number, and then I waited for him to pick up.

Chapter 16

"Croft here," the sheriff said promptly.

"Sheriff, this is Victoria Nelson."

"Victoria, how's your stay at the Pickle Palace going?" he asked.

"Greg told me you came by last night. We've got a problem out here, Sheriff."

"What happened?"

"Curtis's business manager, a man named Christopher Crane, vanished this morning."

"Take it easy," he said. "Vanished is a pretty strong word. Give me some details."

"When he didn't come down for breakfast, Curtis's sister sent the butler off looking for him. He came back a few minutes later and told us that Crane was gone. When we went to his room, it was pretty clear that there had been a struggle, and we found a few drops of blood on the floor of the bathroom."

"Okay, now you've got my attention. How contaminated is the scene?"

"What do you mean?"

He sighed, letting a hint of his exasperation come out. "Did you *all* traipse through the room? Is there *any* chance that I'll get any evidence?"

"The butler was the only one who went in," I said. "I made sure that everyone else stayed out, and I have him guarding the door until you get here."

"I suppose that's more than I should expect," he said.

If it was praise, it was slight indeed. "Will you come out and investigate?"

"You know, there might be a perfectly reasonable explanation for this," the sheriff said. "He might be a uneasy sleeper, or maybe he just left in a hurry. It doesn't necessarily mean that he was abducted."

"What about the blood, then?"

"How much are we talking about here? A little, or a lot?"

"There were at least a few drops that I could see from the hallway," I said.

"He could have cut himself shaving, or maybe he nicked a finger on something sharp. It might not be as ominous as you're making it out to be."

I felt deflated by his suppositions. "Does that mean that you're not even coming out to see for yourself?"

"No, I'll be there in twenty minutes," the sheriff said. "Truth be told, I was heading out your way anyway. Most of my suspects are gathered there, and I was just looking for an excuse to speak with them. Have you done any snooping yourself yet?"

"A little," I admitted. I didn't really want to get into too many details. "Since you discovered that Curtis was murdered, I figured that you'd come out here yesterday."

"I was starting to, and then I got a few phone calls from some folks higher up the food chain than I am. Curtis Trane was a very important man, and I was told to handle things as delicately as possible. That included giving the family a little time alone with their grief. I didn't like it, but there was nothing I could do about it. Besides, I knew that you were already there."

"Is that an endorsement for what Moose and I do?" I asked. If it was, it was a first. Mostly the sheriff left us alone when we were investigating, and that's the way that we liked it.

"Hardly. I just figured that you could do some of the groundwork. If you and your grandfather butted into their lives last night, I had a feeling that they'd be glad to see me today."

"I don't even know how to answer that," I said.

"Then don't. See you soon."

After he hung up, I handed the phone back to Moose, since he'd come back during our conversation.

"What did he say?" my grandfather asked.

"He's on his way. Is there any chance that you'd be willing to postpone breakfast a little longer?"

Moose frowned. "I'm not all that thrilled about it, but if you've got a good reason, I suppose that I can go along with it."

"We need to examine what we found in Curtis's room right now. When Sheriff Croft gets here, I want to be able to turn it all over directly to him."

"Wow, are we really cooperating *that* much these days?" Moose asked me with wonder.

"I figure that it's the least we can do if we want to keep hanging around here without him breathing down our necks. What do you say?"

"Lead on," he said.

We got back to my room, and I was pleased to see that it hadn't been searched since we were gone, at least not to the point that I could tell that it had happened. "Now, where's our stash?" I asked Moose once the door was closed behind us.

My grandfather walked to the big comfy chair and lifted up the seat. "I stuffed it all under here."

"Wouldn't someone look there?" I asked as we retrieved everything.

"Look around, Victoria. Where else could I have put it all? I have a feeling that if I'd jammed it under the bed, the maid might find it, let alone anyone digging into our investigation." He looked at the stash, and then my grandfather grinned at me. "Besides, it appears that everything is still here."

"Then let's spread it all out on the bed and see what we can discover."

Moose did as I asked, and soon enough I was looking down at the checkbook ledger, the old letters, the diary, and the four notebooks filled with odd expressions he'd found.

"Where do you want to start?" Moose asked me.

"I'd like to look at the checks he wrote lately," I said as I reached for the ledger.

"Good. I'll take the diary."

"Are you looking for something scandalous?" I asked my grandfather.

"I'm looking for a motive for murder," he replied, and I felt contrite for a moment until he added, "If I happen to find something juicy, it will just be a bonus."

I flipped through the ledger, and I saw that Sarah had just gotten a check for twenty thousand dollars after all, but there were no entries for Tristan. Could that have been a motive for murder? We'd have to ask them both about that. That wasn't all, though. The day before he'd died, Curtis had written Crane a check for twenty-five thousand dollars. That was odd enough, but the line explaining it was even more striking.

It said, "Final Payment."

What on earth was that supposed to mean?

I would love to ask Crane about it, but first we had to find him.

When I looked up, I saw that Moose was staring at me. "What's wrong?" I asked.

"I've seen that expression on your face before, Victoria. You found something, didn't you?"

"Two things, actually." I showed him the entries, and the lack of one for Tristan. "What do you think about that?"

"I believe that things have just gotten more complicated. Good work holding onto the ledger."

"Thanks. Have you had any luck?"

"It's just a food journal," Moose said with clear disappointment. "The man wrote down every meal that he ate in the last two years. Maybe he did it even longer, but that's as far as this journal goes." My grandfather flung it down on the bed. "What a waste of time."

As it landed, I saw something flutter out and fall to the floor. After I bent down to pick it up, I saw that it was a receipt from a restaurant in Molly's Corners named Joshua's, and from the size of the amount, at least two people had to have eaten there, given Curtis's near lack of appetite as of late. The most telling part of all was the date.

It was for the evening before he was murdered.

Had he dined with his killer the night before he'd died? Had something been said during that meal that had ultimately triggered his death? We were generating more questions than answers as we worked, and I couldn't help wondering if something we'd found so far would ultimately lead us to the murderer. If it did, it seemed as though it wasn't going to be a straight path, but then again, it never was.

I showed the receipt to my grandfather. "Did he eat with his killer the night before he died?" I asked.

"I don't know. I'm going to call Deb and find out, though."

"Who's Deb?" I asked.

"Deb Pence has owned Joshua's for years. We're old friends."

I'd known a great many of the people my grandfather was friends with, but this name was new to me. "Would Martha approve of you contacting her?" I asked him pointedly.

"Relax," Moose said. "That's how I met Deb. She and your grandmother were friends first."

"Good. I just don't want to dig up another Judge Dixon."

Moose got a little flustered whenever I mentioned Holly Dixon's name. The judge and my grandmother didn't get along, all because of a past that Holly and Moose may or may not have shared. It was all long ago, but that didn't mean a thing to Martha. She was the sweetest woman on earth, but she was most definitely not a fan of the judge. "Victoria, you're skating on thin ice."

"That's okay, I'm a born risk-taker, remember? I favor my paternal grandfather in that respect, or so I've been told. You can't fault me for a trait that you passed on to me yourself, Moose."

He wanted to say something biting, but in the end, he couldn't bring himself to do it. "Let's move on, shall we? I don't know how much longer we have before Sheriff Croft gets here. I'll call Deb a little bit later when we've got more time."

I reached for the letters we'd pulled out of Curtis's room, but Moose got to them before I could. "How about splitting them with me?" I asked.

"You can look at the notebooks," he answered with a grin. "After all, you got the checkbook ledger."

"True," I said as I reached for one of the notebooks. As I flipped through the pages, I saw a long list of platitudes and wondered just how much time Curtis had spent thinking them up and dutifully recording them. Every entry was dated, so I searched the books until I found one that was only partially full. Flipping directly to the last few entries, I found a few interesting little tidbits recorded during the last few days of Curtis's life.

The worst enemies are the ones disguised as friends.

Blood may be thicker than water, but a close knife can cut the deepest.

Trust has to be earned, not inherited.

Family is a matter of the heart, not the head.

And finally,

It is better to die alone than live with betrayal.

They weren't happy thoughts by any means, but I hoped that we could at least give Curtis what peace we could by solving his murder. He'd died without being able to trust those closest to him if his final thoughts were any indication, but he'd put his faith in my grandfather and me, and we weren't about to let him down.

Not if it took everything that we had.

"These are all ancient," Moose said as he put the letters back on the bed. "Evidently he dated a girl named Teresa from West Virginia when he was in college, and their breakup was a bad one. He tried to apologize and win her back, but she sent every letter he wrote to her back to him." Moose showed me one of the envelopes, and I saw the date was from far in the past.

"How sad," I said as I reached for one of the letters.

"Take my advice and don't read them," Moose said, his voice choking a little as he spoke. "They're pretty tough to take. Curtis really put his heart out there."

"I can't believe that he kept them all of these years," I said.

"It's funny what latches onto your heart. I wonder if Teresa knows that Curtis is dead? Should we track her down and tell her?"

"It's a sweet thought, but from what you said, it's pretty clear that Curtis has already been dead to her for a long time."

"How about you?" Moose asked as he brushed at the corner of his eye. "Did you find anything?"

I showed him Curtis's last few entries.

Moose whistled softly, and then he said, "Man, talk about sad. He didn't trust anyone in the end, did he?"

"That's not true. He gave Jeffrey power over his estate, and he asked us to solve his murder. I'm going to take some comfort in the fact that at least there were three people he could turn to before he died."

"And we're making one of them a suspect," Moose said.

"We don't have any choice," I said.

"I know, but I don't have to like it." My grandfather looked down at the bed and asked, "Are we finished here?"

"With the time we've got left, I think we've done all that we can do."

"Then let's get this all ready to hand over to Sheriff Croft," Moose said as he gathered everything up into a neat little pile. "I keep wondering something, Victoria."

"What's that?"

"We got a few leads here, but I can't figure out why the killer would risk being discovered to retrieve any of it, can you?"

"I don't know. It does implicate a few of our suspects," I said.

"Maybe so, but there's no real proof in any of it, is there?"

"Perhaps the killer didn't know that. We might not have hit a home run, but I'm still glad I hid everything before I went to sleep last night."

"So am I," Moose said. "Hey, you never told me what you found in that secret passageway. Did you have any luck?"

"As a matter of fact I did," I said. I was about to tell him what I'd overheard when there was a knock at my door.

"Victoria, are you in there?"

It was a familiar voice, and one that I'd been expecting.

"Come in," I said, and the sheriff opened the door and stepped inside.

Chapter 17

"I can't believe you two," Sheriff Croft said in exasperation after Moose and I brought him up to date on what we'd found, and what we'd uncovered during our conversations with our suspects. I left out what I'd heard eavesdropping on Tristan and Sarah in the secret passageway, since I hadn't even shared that with my grandfather yet. "Why don't I go ahead and deputize you both and just get it over with?"

"*Somebody* had to investigate," Moose said.

"I told you before what held me up," the sheriff said. "It took me this long to get permission to come here and even ask questions. But then that's *my* job, isn't it?"

"We both know that, but you really should be thanking us instead of chewing us out," I said. "If it weren't for us, none of this evidence would have even been here. Do you honestly think that Charlotte was really in his room looking for a book? She was there searching for something, and if it hadn't been for us, I have no doubt that she would have found it. As for the rest of them, I don't have any problem imagining any of them going through his room. It would have been like Grand Central Station in there."

"Okay, take it easy. I get your point." The sheriff sat down on one of the chairs with the evidence we'd found on his lap. "This is good work. Even I have to admit that. I guess I'm just frustrated having my hands tied."

"I understand. Thank you," I said.

"You're welcome," he said with a hint of a smile. "This is a political bombshell. It appears that the Trane family has more influence than I thought. I really have to tiptoe around this family."

"How about Crane? Have you checked his room yet?"

The sheriff nodded. "I went there before I came to see

you two," he replied.

"What do you think? Was it foul play?"

"I don't have any idea at this point," he said.

"What about the blood?" Moose asked.

"Like I said on the phone, he could have done that shaving. As for the room being wrecked, I've seen worse."

"That still doesn't explain where he is now, and why he disappeared," I said.

"I've got some of my people out looking for him," the sheriff said, "but for now, there's no reason to suspect that he just didn't get tired of staying here and left on his own."

"What about his car?" Moose asked. "Has anyone looked for that?"

"It's still parked in front of his house," the sheriff said. "Jeffrey brought him here in the limo, so we can assume that he either took a taxi back or he's on foot."

"Have you followed up on that?" I asked.

The sheriff nodded. "There are no record of any pickups here today that we can find. Who knows? Maybe he called a friend to pick him up. These things take time."

"Crane might not have all that much time left," I said.

"Don't be so melodramatic," the sheriff said. "Nine chances out of ten, he'll show up and be surprised about the fuss being made over him."

"Maybe so, but it's the tenth time that I'm worried about," I said.

"Like I said, I'm looking into it." He waved the documents around in the air. "I need to speak with your list of suspects. There are some questions I need answered."

"Good luck with that," Moose said. "They are all pretty good at avoiding anything that even resembles a direct question."

"You don't have to worry about me. I have my own methods of questioning suspects," the sheriff said when his radio squawked, calling his name.

"Croft here," he said.

"Sheriff, we need you back in town pronto."

"I'm busy out here, Melinda," he said. "Is it important?"

"I think so. Someone just fired a shot into the mayor's house," the dispatcher said.

"Was anyone hurt?"

"Apparently His Honor got hit. His wife, Missy, called it in, and she was so hysterical, I couldn't make any sense out of anything she was saying. She kept screaming, "Frank's been shot. Frank's been shot." As of this second, I don't know anything else yet. You'd better get over there ASAP."

"I'm on my way," the sheriff said, and then he turned to us as he headed for the door. "Sorry, but I have to go."

"What about the murder investigation?" Moose asked.

"You heard what Melinda said. An active shooting takes precedence over a victim that's already dead, and it looks like I've got a shooter on the loose in Jasper Fork."

Sheriff Croft was gone before either one of us could even reply. "Moose, who would want to kill Frank Unger?"

"Nobody that I can think of. What's this world coming to?"

"I don't know. Things do seem to be more violent these days than I can remember."

"Maybe *you* can't remember bad times from the past, but I can recall plenty of them," Moose said. "I don't know if things really are getting worse, or if we just hear about them more these days with all of the instant communication we have."

"I don't know." I looked at my hands for a second, and then I asked my grandfather, "What are we supposed to do in the meantime?"

"I'd say that we *have* to keep digging," he said. "The sheriff's going to have his hands full for a while, and somebody needs to keep investigating Curtis's murder."

"It would have made it a whole lot easier if he *had* deputized us," I said.

"I don't think so. I like it just fine not having to deal with any of the rules and regulations that restrict him. After all, we don't need *anyone's* permission to solve Curtis's murder."

"That's true," I said.

"Victoria, I'm all for doing more snooping, but if I don't eat something soon, I'm going to pass out from hunger," Moose said.

"Don't you think that you might be exaggerating just a little?" I asked.

"If anything, I'm understating the situation," he said.

"Give me one more minute, and then we'll go," I said.

"What can't wait until *after* I eat?" Moose asked.

"I thought you might like to learn what I overheard while I was in that secret passageway, but if you want to wait until after we eat, that's fine with me."

Moose looked surprised by my comment. "When you didn't say anything to the sheriff about it, I just assumed that you hit a blank wall."

"I did, but there was a hidden door in the passageway that opened up onto a viewing area," I said. "I was about to walk out when I overheard Tristan and Sarah talking."

"What did they say?" he asked eagerly.

"Are you *sure* you don't want to wait until after breakfast?" I asked him with a grin.

"Victoria, don't toy with a hungry old man."

"Fine. Tristan was worried about us, but Sarah was more concerned about what Jeffrey and Crane might do to hurt them."

"Hurt them? In what way?"

"I never got the chance to find out. They're up to something, though."

"Where exactly did that passageway end?" my grandfather asked me.

"It opened up into the hallway landing where we spoke to everyone last night when we came out of Curtis's room," I said.

"That's too bad," Moose answered.

"Why is that?"

"Think about it, Victoria. I was hoping that it would lead

directly to someone else's room. At least that way we've have a good idea about who visited you last night. If the passageway goes into the hall, *anyone* could have accessed it."

"If they knew that it was there in the first place," I said.

"Sure, but we don't have any way to discover who knew about the passageway and who didn't, do we?" he asked.

"Is there any way that we can block the entrance into my room?" I asked as I glanced over at the panel.

"It opens inward, so I don't see how. It really bothers you, doesn't it?"

"Wouldn't it irk you?" I asked. "I just don't feel safe here."

"Maybe that's a good thing," Moose said. "If we're both on our toes all of the time, we have a better chance of making it out of here alive."

"The killer doesn't have any reason to come after us now, right?"

"I don't know about that," Moose said as he scratched his chin. "After all, we're asking a lot of pointed questions, and they might not like us digging into what happened to Curtis. If we get too close, we could become a threat they feel they have to deal with."

"I wish we were," I said. "Right now I feel as though we're just spinning our wheels."

"It's not all that bad," Moose said. "After all, we've got some angles to explore with our suspects, and there's always the fact that Crane has vanished altogether."

"Do you think that means that he's the one who killed Curtis?"

My grandfather shrugged. "It doesn't *necessarily* mean that, but if he left of his own volition, he might be up to *something*. Think about it. He didn't look all that comfortable about having Renee here last night, did he?"

"No, it was pretty clear that the news of her involvement wasn't something that he was all that happy to learn about. Would that alone make him run?"

"If he *was* cooking the books, having a forensic accountant examine them is probably the worst thing that he could imagine happening," Moose said. "Then again, it could all be innocent."

"You don't believe that any more than I do," I said. "It has to mean something."

"Yeah, more than likely it does. We just don't know what yet."

"Then let's get a quick bite of breakfast and then see if we can find out," I said.

"Finally, we get to eat," Moose said with a grin.

"I have a feeling that it's the *only* way that I'm going to get you to stop talking about food," I answered.

"You're hungry, too; admit it."

"I could eat," I said, and then I smiled as I opened my door.

To my surprise, I nearly ran over someone standing just on the other side of it. Had she been trying to listen in on my conversation with my grandfather?

"Sarah, what are you doing here?" I asked.

She frowned in reply. "I was sent to fetch you both."

"Why didn't you just knock, then?" Moose asked her as we all started downstairs.

"I was about to when Victoria opened the door and saved me the trouble," Sarah said. Why didn't I believe her?

"What do you need?"

"Aunt Charlotte insists that you join us, and no one gets to eat until you do."

I understood that the household followed certain rules, but I couldn't believe that they'd actually been waiting for us this long before they'd eat. If it were too much longer, we'd all be having lunch. "We were just on our way down."

"Good," she said. "What did that cop have to say?"

"The sheriff?" Moose asked.

"How many cops were here? Of course I mean the sheriff."

"He just wanted to touch base with us," I said casually.

"Do you know why he left so quickly?" Sarah asked.

"He had an emergency," Moose answered. "But don't worry. He'll be back."

Why did I get the impression that Sarah wasn't all that pleased with the news? She quickly masked it, though. "Good to know."

We walked into the dining room, and sure enough, Jeffrey was still sitting there, along with Tristan and Charlotte.

"Sorry we're late," I said as I took my seat again.

Moose added, "Me, too," as he joined us.

Charlotte didn't even comment as she reached for the bell and rang it. The food came immediately, and I expected it to be cold and just about inedible, but to my surprise, it was all hot and fresh. Everything must have been thrown out and they'd started over. I was certain that hadn't endeared any of us with Chef Cassidy, but it couldn't be helped.

As we ate, Charlotte made a few attempts at polite conversation, but after everyone pretty much ignored her, she gave up, and we mostly ate in peace.

After we finished, Tristan asked me, "So, what's on your agenda today?"

"My grandfather and I have a few things that we need to do," I said. "How about you?"

"I'll be in my studio all morning. I'm painting Sarah."

His sister rolled her eyes. "Must we do that today, given all that's happened around here lately, Tristan?"

"I think it might be a welcome relief to both of us to have something to do to occupy our time," he said. "It will keep our minds off what happened to Uncle Curtis."

"Sitting on a stool holding a parasol isn't exactly all that absorbing to me," she protested. "It might be different if it ended up looking *anything* like me, but you might as well be painting an umbrella stand as much as it's going to resemble me by the time you're finished."

"I'm trying to capture your inner spirit," Tristan said, clearly offended by his sister's criticism.

"Well, you need to keep looking, because when I peeked at it yesterday, it wasn't anywhere close by."

"You have to be patient," he said. "These things take time. Besides, you promised."

"Fine," she said with a snort.

"How about you, Charlotte?" Moose asked.

"He keeps asking me, but I refuse to pose for him on general principle alone," she answered.

"That's not what I meant," Moose said. "What are you going to do today?"

"I have work to do, real work," she said.

"Will you be able to do it from here?" I asked.

"Why do you ask?"

"It will help if we have access to all of you in case we need to talk to you," I said. "We're taking Curtis's last request to us quite seriously."

"Just as you should," Jeffrey said. "I'm sure that everyone will be delighted to continue to cooperate with you both."

"Of course we will," Charlotte said as she shot Jeffrey a quick glare.

I was bracing myself for his reply when Humphries appeared with a familiar face in tow. "Ms. West has arrived," he said, and Renee stepped forward.

"I'm sorry. I didn't mean to interrupt your breakfast," she said. "I can come back later."

"Nonsense," Jeffrey said with a grin. "I was finished, anyway. I'm afraid that it's just going to be the two of us, though."

"What happened to Crane?" she asked with a frown.

"That's what we're still trying to determine," he replied. "Come on, I'll explain on the way."

She nodded in my direction and smiled, and then she did the same with Moose as she and Jeffrey walked away.

"If you'll excuse us as well," I said as I stood.

"Of course," Charlotte replied.

We all left the dining room then, my grandfather and me in one direction, the brother and sister leaving together in another, and Charlotte heading off to who knew where by herself.

That just left my grandfather and me.

It was time to start digging anew.

Chapter 18

"Where should we start today?" I asked Moose as we walked out into the foyer together.

"The first thing that I need to do is call Deb Pence at Joshua's," he said as he reached for his cellphone.

He looked frustrated a few seconds later.

"Is something wrong?" I asked.

"I can't get a signal here," he said. "I'm going to walk out onto the porch and see if I can do any better there."

I was about to walk out with him when I saw Humphries lingering behind the stairs. I was certain that he thought that he was out of my line of sight, but he'd shifted at precisely the wrong moment, and I'd spotted him.

"I'll be right there," I whispered.

Moose raised an eyebrow, and I pointed toward where the butler was hiding. He nodded, and then my grandfather stepped outside alone.

I walked straight to Humphries's hiding place. "Are you lurking?" I asked him with a smile.

He didn't even look embarrassed by being caught eavesdropping. "It's my job to be invisible, but available at all times."

"Wow, that must be tough to do," I said.

"It can be challenging at times. Is there something I can do for you?"

I nodded. "You can answer a question for me. What do *you* think happened to Crane?"

He looked surprised to hear me ask him. "I'm sure that I don't know."

"That's the thing. *None* of us know, but I have a hunch that you have an *opinion*."

The butler looked uncomfortable. "I'm not accustomed to being directly asked my opinion about anything."

"Then think of this as your lucky day," I said.

He thought about my question, and then Humphries said, "I think he left of his own volition."

"That's interesting. Why do you say that?"

"If he were dragged away, *someone* would have heard him," Humphries said. "I'm not the only one listening in to the heartbeat of this house."

"Who else might have heard something?" I asked.

"It's well known that Ms. Trane has insomnia," he said softly. "She doesn't miss much."

"You don't care for her a great deal, do you?"

Humphries took a step back. "I'm sure that I don't know what you mean. She is a delight." The stone expression on his face made me realize that I'd overstepped my boundaries with him this time. There was a fine line between having a confidential conversation and showing loyalty to his employers, and though Charlotte wasn't his boss directly, she was still Curtis Trane's sister.

"I'm sorry. I didn't mean to say that. Forgive me."

Humphries looked surprised. "There's no need to apologize."

"Clearly there is," I said. "If it were you, how would you go about finding Crane?"

"I'm sure that I wouldn't know."

There was a barrier that was up now in full force, and I wasn't having any luck breaking through it, at least not at the moment. He'd been more open to talking with me before I'd asked him about Charlotte Trane, but that door had slammed shut. I'd try him again later, or maybe even have Moose make a run at questioning the butler, but for now, Humphries was just another dead end.

I was still trying to come up with something to break the ice again when Moose walked in and the door closed loudly behind him. "Sorry about that." He spotted me talking to Humphries and walked over toward us. "There you are," he said.

Before Moose could reach us, the butler said, "If you'll

excuse me, I must go."

"We'll chat again later," I called out after him hopefully, but he didn't even look back.

"Wow, what did you *say* to him, Victoria?"

"We were getting along just fine, and then I asked him how he felt about Charlotte Trane, and he turned to stone on me."

Moose shook his head. "Of course he did. She's the only reference here that he has left. It's going to be tough enough finding another high-end servant's job for him as it is, given his history. Humphries can't afford to have any bad comments coming from a member of the Trane family."

"Maybe you can pump him for more information later yourself," I said.

"Sure, but let's give him a little time."

"What did Deb have to say?"

Moose frowned. "I never got her. She's not due in until three this afternoon."

"I wouldn't mind having those hours," I said.

"Not me. She probably works until after midnight, and I for one like my beauty sleep," Moose said with a grin.

"We can both use all of *that* we can get," I answered. "So, I suppose that we'll have to wait to find out who Curtis ate with the night before he died."

"If Deb even knows," Moose said. "There's a chance that no one noticed, or even if they did, they might not be able to identify his dining companion."

"Worse yet, even if someone at the restaurant can name names, there are no guarantees that it even had anything to do with his murder."

My grandfather smiled. "That's just part of the joy of investigating, isn't it?"

"You like it. Admit it."

"I love the challenge of it," my grandfather admitted, "but I hate that we don't get involved unless we lose someone who has touched our lives."

"It's what motivates us, though," I said. "I'm guessing

that we're not going to sit around waiting for Deb to call you back."

"Hardly, but where does that leave us?"

I thought about it, and then I said, "I think we should speak directly with the lawyer who amended Curtis's will," I said. "I'd love to know what changes he was going to make before someone stopped him."

"Whoever it is, he's not going to tell us anything."

"That might be true, but he'll tell Jeffrey, don't you think?" I asked as I started for the library.

"There's only one way to find out," Moose said.

We found the chauffeur sitting at the table studying a document in front of him. Renee was leaning over his shoulder, touching him lightly, as she peered at it as well. There was no hint of impropriety, but that didn't keep her from jerking up and away from him when we walked in. Was Jeffrey blushing a little?

"What can I do for you?" Jeffrey asked as he shuffled a few papers on the library table.

"Have you seen the will?" I asked him.

"It's here somewhere," Jeffrey said as he nodded. Renee helped him search, and a few seconds later, she pulled a thick document from the pile. "Got it."

"May we see it?" I asked Jeffrey.

"Of course," he said.

I took the will and saw that it was dated two years before. I started scanning through it, searching for beneficiaries. When I found the right section, I found that Charlotte inherited half the money, while Tristan and Sarah split the other half. I showed it to Moose, who was still reading it as I asked, "Is there any chance we can find out what Curtis's new will said, the one he hadn't signed yet?"

"I don't know," Jeffrey said. "I'm not sure that he'll tell me."

"Of course he will," Renee said. "You're the estate executor. There's a great deal of power associated with that.

I'm certain that if you call and ask, he'll tell you anything that you want to know."

"Honestly?" Jeffrey asked. "That's all that it will take?"

"Jeffrey, your position is to act as Curtis's representative. This is not the time to be timid."

"Let me give him a call then," Jeffrey said.

As he made the phone call, I said softly to Renee, "How's it going?"

"Slowly but surely," she said with a smile. "I don't know whether to thank you or curse you for bringing me in on this."

"It's your own fault, you know," I said with a grin of my own.

"What makes you say that?"

"If you didn't want to me to call you, you shouldn't be so good at what you do."

"Guilty as charged," she said. "Honestly, though, it is fascinating. Curtis Trane left an amazingly complex estate behind."

"It's hard to believe that it all started with pickles," I said, remembering my late friend's penchant for giving away little plastic pickles.

"It may have started that way, but he's a long way from that now. The estate owns an interest in the Charlotte football team, did you know that?"

"I didn't have a clue," I said.

"It's in here, and so is his minority ownership in the North Carolina Philharmonic. The man had his fingers in dozens upon dozens of pies in the state. It's going to take years to straighten it all out."

"You just smiled as you said that," I said.

"What can I say? I've always loved a challenge."

I looked over at Jeffrey, whose face had gone white all of sudden as the telephone dropped out of his hands.

"Are you okay?" I asked him softly, concerned for the man's health.

Jeffrey shook his head from side to side, nodded, and then

he shook his head again. What was that supposed to mean? As he picked the telephone back up and continued to speak, he grew more and more ashen, and I was beginning to wonder if we should call a doctor for him. It was quite cryptic trying to make sense of the conversation based strictly on his part of it, and when he finally hung up, I was even more concerned about him.

"Is it really all that bad?" I asked him.

"I need some water," he croaked out.

I reached for the pitcher, but Renee was quicker. She poured some hastily and handed him the glass. Jeffrey's hands were shaking as he took it, and after gulping some of it down, he promptly started choking. Moose patted him hard on the back, a move I wondered about, but it cleared up soon enough.

"Are you all right?" Renee asked.

"I think so," he said, his voice a little hoarse from his recent ordeal.

"What did he say that shook you up so much?" I asked him.

"I don't even know where to begin," Jeffrey said.

"I've always found that the beginning is as good a place to start as any," Moose said.

"It appears that Curtis signed a new will after all just before he was murdered," Jeffrey said ominously.

Chapter 19

"Oh, no," I said. "Are you out as the executor now?"

"No, as a matter of fact, the only thing in the entire document that Curtis changed was his list of beneficiaries," Jeffrey said.

"I didn't think he had time to change it," Moose said.

"That's what everyone thought, but the attorney came by late the night before Curtis was murdered and brought a few witnesses with him. I *wondered* why he sent me out for a quart of black cherry ice cream. He must not have wanted me to know about it."

"Why would he hide it from you?" Renee asked.

"Evidently because I'm in the new will," Jeffrey said.

"That's sweet of him to remember you," I said. "You were a good friend to him all the way to the end. It should give you some real comfort knowing that he thought just as fondly of you as you did of him. Will it be enough to make a difference in your life?"

"You could say that," Jeffrey said. "He left me everything."

Chapter 20

"He did what?" I asked. "Are you serious?"

"Evidently it's true," Jeffrey said. "I can't *believe* that he did that."

Was it possible that the chauffeur was *upset* about the latest twist? "Jeffrey, aren't you *happy* about it?" I asked him.

"It's no wonder that he sent me out and kept this from me. If he'd breathed one word of it to me beforehand, I would have left on the spot."

"Why would you do that?" Moose asked. "It's what he wanted, after all."

"You don't understand. The three of us were the only people in his life that he considered his real friends, not people bought and paid for," Jeffrey said. "He tried to triple my salary three weeks ago, and I flatly refused. As a matter of fact, I made him give me a cut in pay, or I threatened to go on strike," Jeffrey added with a grin. "It wasn't about the money, not in the past year, anyway."

"You could just give it all away if you wanted to," Renee said, her first input into the conversation since Jeffrey first dropped the bombshell.

"Is that what you think I should do?" he asked her intently.

"Hang on a second here," I said. "Let's not make any crazy decisions just yet."

Renee stopped me with an icy glare. "Victoria, I believe that Jeffrey just asked me a question, and if it's all the same to you, I'd like to answer it."

"Sorry," I said. It wasn't really any of my business. I just hated seeing him throw away such a vast fortune just to make a point of his loyalty to his late employer.

"It's okay," she said with a smile before she turned back

to Jeffrey. “Victoria is right about one thing. You need to think this through before you do *anything*. There’s a great deal of good you can do with the resources we’re talking about here.”

“That’s true,” he said. “I never thought about it that way.”

“Perhaps you should,” she said. “Besides, it’s not in your pocket yet, not by any stretch of the imagination. I have a feeling that the family isn’t going to accept this without fighting you first.”

“You’re right about that,” Jeffrey said with a grin. “Curtis would have relished the battle; I’m sure of that much. Okay, for now, we’ll just proceed as we have been. After all, in the end it doesn’t matter who inherits Curtis’s estate. All that we need to worry about is straightening out this mess of paperwork.”

“It matters a little,” Moose said softly, but I didn’t think anyone else heard it.

“What was that?” Jeffrey asked.

“Not important. Can I ask you for a favor, Jeffrey?”

“Anything,” he said.

Moose grinned. “You need to be very careful now about saying that.” Funny, I’d given him the exact same advice earlier, but it meant a great deal more now that he was going to be rich.

“Note taken,” he said. “What can I do for you?”

“It’s not really a favor; it’s more like a piece of advice. I wouldn’t be in any hurry to tell the others about this new development.”

“That’s not a bad idea,” Renee said. “There’s no use stirring up any more trouble at the moment than you’ve already got on your hands. You have enough to deal with as it is.”

“Okay, I can see that. We’ll just keep this between ourselves for the time being.”

“We’ll leave you to your books, then,” I said.

As Moose and I left them, I couldn’t help but notice that it mattered to someone else, too.

Renee was a good three feet away from Jeffrey now, a dramatic change since he'd learned that he was going to be rich beyond all dreams of avarice. I hoped that she didn't let that put a stumbling block between them, but I promised myself that I'd butt out and leave them to figure it out for themselves.

Unless they made the wrong decision, of course.

"We need to talk to Sarah," I told my grandfather once we left Renee and Jeffrey.

"You're thinking about that checkbook ledger entry, aren't you?"

"I think it's interesting that she got twenty thousand dollars, but Tristan didn't," I said. "That's a lot of money."

"Maybe for us," Moose said, "but was it much more than pocket change for Curtis?"

"He might have been rich, but I don't think that he ever *threw* it away."

"If Sarah is still posing for her brother, should we wait until they're apart to ask her about it?" Moose asked me.

"Actually, we *might* get better results if we ask her in *front* of Tristan," I said.

My grandfather smiled at me. "You never were afraid to stir the pot, were you?"

"I just think we have a better chance of seeing their true characters if we press them together. Who knows? Maybe there's a perfectly reasonable explanation for it."

"I'm looking forward to hearing it," Moose said.

Humphries was in the hallway, so I called out to him, "Do you have a second?"

"Certainly," he said.

"Where might we find Tristan and Sarah?"

The butler frowned before he answered. "Mr. Wellborne doesn't like to be disturbed while he's working. He can be quite emphatic about it."

"Don't worry. We won't tell him how we found him," I said.

Humphries nodded. "His studio is in the loft above the garage. It has its own separate staircase."

"I thought Jeffrey's apartment was above the garage," I said.

"It is, but he only has a small portion of it, hardly bigger than a closet. The main space is Mr. Wellborne's art studio."

It was ironic that Jeffrey had been living in such a small space before, and now he was going to own everything of value around him, including a great deal of square footage. "Thank you, Humphries," I said.

"For what?" he asked with a slight smile.

Moose grinned in return. "That's right, Victoria. I'm sorry that Humphries couldn't help us, too. We'll just have to find Tristan and Sarah on our own."

"Why don't we look above the garage?" I said, getting into the spirit of things.

"It's as good a place to begin as any," my grandfather said.

Humphries managed a smile as we walked past him. Maybe I'd made amends, but I wasn't about to press him soon about anything.

Moose and I walked outside, and the dark clouds above us were again ominous. It had been raining, storming, or just about to rain or storm since we'd gotten to the Pickle Palace, and there was a small, albeit irrational part of me that thought it was Curtis showing his anger from the great beyond about being murdered. It was nonsense, of course, but I still couldn't help thinking it.

A set of iron steps ran up one side of the garage, and Moose and I mounted them gingerly. We were about to intentionally irritate two of our suspects, and one of them was possibly a murderer. Hopefully it would get results. We were running out of time, and nobody was more aware of it than we were. Curtis's memorial was scheduled for the next morning, and at that point, we'd lose access to nearly all of our suspects.

It was time to turn up the heat.

"No one is allowed in here while I'm working!" Tristan snapped at my grandfather and me as we walked into the studio uninvited.

"In our defense, we knocked first," I said, trying to be heard over the loud music playing in the background. "Can you turn that down a little?"

"It helps me focus," he said loudly.

Sarah was sitting on a chair holding a parasol and looking absolutely bored to tears. "For heaven's sake, Tristan, it's giving me a headache, too." She stood to turn the music down.

"Sit back down!" he commanded her.

"Then turn the music off," she shouted back.

He did it, although it was clear that it was a reluctant decision on his part. "What do you two want?" he asked as he turned to us. I couldn't see his canvas, and as tempted as I was to walk over and take a peek at it, I decided to fight the impulse.

"We need to speak with Sarah," Moose said.

"She can't be bothered right now. My work is at a critical stage."

"You don't need to *do* anything," I said. "Sarah, would you mind answering a question for us?"

She rolled her eyes. "You two are as bad as my brother."

"What is that supposed to mean?" he asked her as his brush hovered above the canvas.

"Everyone wants *something* from me," she said. Sarah turned to me and asked, "What is it that you want to know?"

"Why did your uncle write you a check for twenty thousand dollars last week?" I asked.

"He what!" Tristan shouted. "That's ridiculous. You must be mistaken."

"We saw the entry in his checkbook ledger ourselves," Moose said matter-of-factly.

"What were you doing looking at that?" Sarah asked,

nicely sidestepping our question. "I was willing to put up with the inconvenience of having you compiling something about my uncle, but you've gone too far. There's no reason at all for you to look through his personal things."

She wasn't about to put me off that easily. "We have Jeffrey's full approval for everything that we're doing," I said. "If you have any problem with that, you'll have to take it up with him."

"I will," Sarah said as she stood again.

"Sarah!" Tristan snapped.

"Oh stuff it, dear brother," she said as she threw down the parasol that she'd been holding. "I'm tired of this."

As she walked straight at him, he tried to stop her. "It's not ready yet."

"Too bad. I've at least earned the right to look at what you've been doing." She pushed past him and then stood in front of the canvas for a full ten seconds before she spoke. "*This* is what you've been doing all of this time? Are you *kidding* me?"

It was too good a chance to pass up, so I walked toward the canvas as well. I got there before Moose, but not by much. The vivid dabs of paint on his palette, the selection of brushes, the scent of the turpentine, even the structured lines of the canvas and the easel made him look like a real artist.

I wasn't so sure of that when I saw the result of his work.

The canvas sported a series of faintly penciled lines, some parallel and some not, running in all kinds of different directions. Within this grid, there were dabs and splashes of color. Examined up close, it was something a child could do, but as I stepped back, the form on the canvas began to show itself. If I looked at it just so, I could start to see Sarah emerge. Not the girl herself, but a representation of her, at any rate.

"It's rubbish," the model snapped.

"I don't know. I think I see where he's going," I said.

Moose looked at me with a startled expression. "Seriously?"

"Stand back here and look at it," I said.

He did as I asked, but my grandfather still shook his head at the sight. "Sorry, but I don't see it."

"That's because you have a pedestrian eye," Tristan said, and then he turned to me. "Do you really see what I'm striving to achieve?"

"I do," I answered honestly. "I can't wait to see it finished."

"Well, you're going to have to wait a very long time," Sarah said. "I'm finished posing for it."

"You can't," Tristan said. "I need you."

"Sorry," Sarah said as she started to leave. Tristan may have been completely distracted by his sister's actions and my comments, but I couldn't afford to let it happen to me.

I stepped in front of Sarah. "Why did he write you that check?"

"It's none of your business," she said.

"I already told you. It's my business now," I said.

"I want to know the answer to that question myself," Tristan said. Was he backing me because he really wanted to know, or was he just returning the favor? As long as it worked for me, I didn't particularly care.

"We made a bet, and he lost," Sarah said.

"That's a lie," I said. "Curtis hated gambling." I remembered Jeffrey's comments about his own debts, and his reluctance to discuss them with his employer and friend.

"That's true," Tristan said. "What's going on, Sarah?"

"It was for my ex, okay? Are you happy now?" she asked as she glared at me.

"What about him?" Tristan asked.

"He threatened to post some embarrassing video of us together on the Internet if I didn't pay him, and Uncle Curtis agreed to help me."

"Why should I believe you?" Tristan asked her.

"Would I have just admitted it to you if it weren't true? Why would I do that, Tristan?"

"Maybe you're hiding something even worse," he said.

Sarah looked at her brother with a sneer, and then moved it on to my grandfather and me. "I don't have to stay here and take this." She narrowed her focus to me as she added, "You need to move."

I looked at Moose, and he just shrugged, so I stepped aside.

Once she was gone, I asked Tristan, "What do you know about her ex-husband?"

"Oh, Nat is a real prize. I wouldn't put it past him for a second."

"How do we find him?" Moose asked him.

"Is it really all that important now?" Tristan asked.

"I'd like to know if it's true," my grandfather said.

Tristan shrugged. "I've still got his number on my phone from when they were married. I can call him for you, if you'd like."

It was odd to have Tristan helping us, but I wasn't about to turn it down. "That would be great. Could you put him on speakerphone?"

"Sure, why not?"

A gruff man picked up on the third ring. "Tris? I never expected to hear from you again."

"Hey, Nat. Listen, I just talked to Sarah—"

"She's lying," he said. "I never asked her for anything."

"Slow down," Tristan said. "At least let me finish."

"And listen to whatever lies she said about me? I don't think so."

"Answer one thing for me first. You owe me that much, or do I need to remind you?"

There was a slight pause, and Nat's voice came back on a little more contrite. "Make it quick."

"Did you at least delete the video like you promised?"

He paused even longer before he answered this time. "If you're taping this, you know that it won't stand up in court."

"It's just us," Tristan said as he made a shushing gesture to Moose and me.

"I promise you that your sister will never hear from me

again." With the weight he used in his words, I believed him. "Do me a favor and lose this number, okay? We're finished, too."

"Done," Tristan said, and he reached out and disconnected the call.

"So, she was telling the truth after all," Tristan said.

"After we pushed her some, it appears that she finally did," Moose said.

"I still wouldn't turn my back on her if I were you two," Tristan said as he turned back to his canvas. "Now, if you'll excuse me, I've got work to do."

"Without your model?" my grandfather asked him.

"I can work from memory for now," he said. Almost absentmindedly, he reached out and turned the music back on, cranking it up to a volume so loud that any further possibility of conversation was over.

We could still hear the bass booming from outside.

"It appears that the interview is over," my grandfather said with a smile. "I was wondering how long your goodwill was going to last. Did you really see something in that train wreck of a painting?"

"I wasn't lying," I said. "I think that it has real potential."

"Victoria, do me a favor; never buy art for me."

"Agreed," I said. "At least we got an explanation for the check Curtis wrote for Sarah."

"It doesn't do anything to clear her of his murder though, does it?"

"No, I'm afraid we're still stuck with our original list of suspects," I said.

"So, who do we go after next?" he asked.

I didn't have a chance to answer, though, because his cellphone rang at that moment.

"This could be important," he said as he answered it, and I held my breath, hoping that we'd finally get a break in the case.

Chapter 21

"Really? Are you sure? Okay, thanks. Yeah, when I can, I will," Moose said. I didn't even know who he was talking to, and his cryptic responses certainly didn't help any. He looked thoughtful as he signed off and put his phone away. "Well, that was interesting."

"Who was it?" I asked.

"Deb finally got my message. She remembers Curtis and his companion, mostly because Curtis barely touched his food, even though he ordered a pretty varied selection off the menu."

"He'd lost his appetite lately," I said. "The only thing he really seemed to enjoy were my mother's pancakes."

"Who could blame him?" Moose asked. "They're pretty wonderful."

"I'm sure that she'd appreciate hearing that, but what else did Deb have to say?"

"Curtis was there with Charlotte. What's more, they had an argument, and she stormed off in the middle of the meal. Evidently she made quite a scene doing it, too."

"That's interesting," I said. "I wonder if they were fighting about him changing his will?"

"It could be," Moose said. "The only way that we're going to be able to find out is if we come right out and ask her."

"Let's go," I said.

At the bottom of the steps of the studio, I noticed Humphries walking purposefully toward us.

"I wonder what's up with him?" Moose asked.

"I don't know, but I have a feeling that it's not good."

"I need you both to come with me right now," the butler said.

"What's the matter? Did we do something wrong?" I

asked. His tone of voice was scolding in nature.
"Ms. Trane wishes to speak with you immediately."
"Wishes, or demands?" Moose asked. "I don't take kindly to being bossed around by anyone but my wife."
"You're not all that fond of that, either," I said, and then I turned to Humphries. "What's really going on?"
"I'm just doing as I've been instructed," he said.
"Lead on, then," I said. "It's a happy coincidence, because we want to talk to her, too."
"I'm afraid this conversation is going to be a little more one-sided than that," Humphries said.
"Charlotte might be under that impression right now, but we're about to show her how wrong she is," I said.
Moose nodded his approval. "This is going to be fun. I'm getting tired of tiptoeing around everyone here."
"Have we been tiptoeing up until now?" I asked him with a smile.
"Just wait and see," he answered.
"Humphries, if I were you, I'd get out of the line of fire as soon as you lead us to Charlotte. I'd hate to be responsible for getting you into trouble," Moose said.
"I'll be fine," he said, and I could swear that I saw a hint of a smile in his face before he quickly shut it down.

"I don't know what you just said to my niece, but she's extremely unhappy with both of you," Charlotte said as we found her holding court in the grand dining room.
"Sorry about that," I said, though it was clear to everyone present that I didn't mean it. "We had to ask some hard questions."
"Are you *still* trying to convince me that all of it was done in the name of this tribute that you are supposedly creating for my late brother?"
"The only fitting way to end it is to find his killer," I said, staring right back at her. I'd faced down more than my share of belligerent customers in my past, and she didn't have anything that I hadn't already seen. In many situations, the

only way to deal with a bully was to back them down.

"That is utterly ridiculous," she said. "What qualifications do you have to even attempt that?"

"We've done it before," Moose said. "Experience is an awfully fine teacher."

"You are both bumbling amateurs, and I've had enough of your snooping and prying into our lives."

"I can understand you feeling that way," Moose said, "but you don't have the final say, now do you?" He was actually enjoying this. Confrontations usually left me a little shaky afterward, but Moose always reveled in a good fight.

"We'll see about that. I'm taking steps to correct that particular miscarriage myself."

"Good luck with that," Moose said. He was being a bit irascible, and I had no desire to get in his way. Sometimes it was the best way to shake things up, and he was clearly on a roll. "You seem kind of upset right now, is that true?"

"Why shouldn't I be?" she asked harshly.

"I get that. I'm just trying to figure out if you're madder now, or when you walked out on Curtis at dinner the night before he died."

There was dead silence in the room.

Charlotte wanted to deny it; I could tell when she took that first deep breath, but evidently she changed her mind before she spoke. Moose knew what had happened, so she could see that there was no use trying to say that it wasn't so. "My brother and I often had words in public," she said. "While it's regrettable that I never got the opportunity to make amends with him, it didn't change how we felt about each other."

It was time for me to step in and offer her a little sympathy at this point. "It must have crushed you losing that chance. What were you arguing about?" I asked in my most understanding voice.

"His plans to distribute his estate," she said. "It's all that we ever argued about lately."

"You didn't care for his proposal?" I asked softly,

searching for a clue whether she knew about Jeffrey's new status or not.

"He was going to give it all away to some *charity*," she said. "That money deserved to stay in the family. After all, the family earned it."

If she was lying, Charlotte was doing a masterful job of it.

"Which charity did he have in mind?" I asked gently.

"Who knows? It changed so often. He couldn't make up his mind about what to do with it all. I suggested that he leave it my hands, and he laughed at me! Can you imagine? He laughed!"

Wow. Charlotte had clearly forgotten who she was talking to for a moment and let her true feelings show. Things were not nearly as peaceful between her and her brother as she'd been trying to lead us to believe. While it was most likely true that she hadn't known about Jeffrey's change in status as the final and lone heir, it was obvious that she didn't approve of Curtis's money going anywhere but his immediate family. Charlotte must have realized how she sounded, because she quickly composed herself again. "My brother loved to goad me into making me lose my temper, and I'm afraid that I succumbed the night before he died. That is something that I'll have to live with for the rest of my life, but it's none of your business. I'm afraid that I'm going to have to ask you both to pack your bags and leave." She said the last bit with all of the weight and authority that being a lifelong Trane gave her.

"I don't think so," a voice said just behind me. I turned to see Jeffrey standing there, Renee by his side.

"You are on thin ice," she said to him coldly. "I am quite tired of your insubordinate attitude, young man."

"Be that as it may," Jeffrey said, "You're going to have to find a way to live with it."

"Perhaps for now," she said, and there was no hiding the threat in her voice now.

Jeffrey didn't even let it touch him. Moose, Renee, and I knew why, but I was certain that Charlotte didn't have a clue.

"That's really all that counts though, isn't it?" Jeffrey asked, and then he turned to my grandfather and me. "I'd appreciate it if you'd stay on another day."

"We're happy to do it," Moose said, and I nodded as well.

Charlotte saw that she'd lost this particular battle, and she wasn't going to fight it anymore, at least for now. "I have important things to see to," she said as she stood and swept regally out of the room.

"What made you come to our rescue?" I asked Jeffrey with the hint of a grin after she was gone.

"Are you kidding? I heard her yelling at you both from down the hall. Are you okay?"

Moose smiled at him. "We get worse than that every day at the diner."

"I'm afraid that we're going to need that extra time, too," I said. "Once the memorial service is over, I have a hunch that everyone is going to be leaving."

"Then you just have to work harder," Jeffrey said. "You can't let anyone leave until you've found out who killed Curtis."

"We're doing our best," I said.

"I'm sure that you are," Jeffrey said as he softened a little.

"How's it coming with you two?" I asked.

"The paperwork is challenging," Renee said.

"I'm sure that it is," I answered. "We're already in the dining room, and breakfast wasn't much. Is anyone else hungry?"

"We could take a break, couldn't we?" Jeffrey asked Renee.

"Whatever you'd like to do is fine with me," she said.

"Then it's settled. I'll get Cassidy to whip us up something special."

"Don't make it anything too fancy," Moose said. "I'd hate to get spoiled."

"I don't know," I added. "I wouldn't mind a little pampering, myself."

"Then let's do it," Jeffrey said.

"That was unbelievable," I said as I pushed my plate away from the table Humphries had set up for us in the library. We'd had brisket, garlic mashed potatoes, and asparagus shoots for the main course, with strawberry shortcake for dessert, and everything had been delicious. It had just been the four of us eating: Jeffrey, Renee, Moose, and me. "I especially enjoyed the company."

"I didn't see any reason to make you eat with the triple threat," Jeffrey said with a grin. "I figured without Tristan, Sarah, and Charlotte, we might not see as much drama as we've been having lately."

"I'm pretty sure that Charlotte isn't going to be happy with you," I said.

"At this point, could she dislike me any more than she already does? I for one don't think so."

I wasn't sure if the power, the money, or a combination of the two had given the chauffeur a new air of confidence, but so far, I liked it.

"You can probably live without a gold star from her, can't you?" Moose asked.

"I'll do my best," he said. Jeffrey then turned to Renee and added, "I couldn't do this without you; you know that, don't you?"

She blushed a little from the praise. "I'm not really doing all that much."

"Don't underestimate what you're bringing to the process," Jeffrey said. "It's really nice having someone like you on my side."

"Don't forget about us," Moose said with a grin. "Or did you remember that we were here, too?"

"I meant…you know…the paperwork." It was Jeffrey's turn to blush a little now.

"Moose," I said as I tapped his arm. "Play nice."

"What?" he asked as his smile blossomed even more.

"Don't pay any attention to him," I said.

"Victoria, he's a grown man. He can take a little ribbing."

"He's right," Jeffrey said. "What are your plans for this afternoon?"

"The first thing I'm going to do is see if my cellphone has charged yet," I said. "I hate to admit it, but I feel kind of naked without it."

"They're handy, aren't they?" Renee said. "Sometimes a little too handy. I've been known to leave mine in my office on occasion just to get a little peace and quiet."

"I understand that," Jeffrey said. "It can be tough always being at someone else's beck and call all of the time."

"You shouldn't have that problem anymore," Moose said.

"Maybe, maybe not," Jeffrey replied.

"What's going on? Has something happened that we're not aware of?" I asked him.

Renee answered for him. "Jeffrey is afraid that Charlotte and her minions will find a way to nullify the most recent will."

"Tell me it hasn't crossed your mind," Jeffrey said. "I keep thinking that this is all too good to be true, and I could be right."

"That's why Starnes is coming by with a copy tomorrow morning," she said reassuringly. "I haven't met the man, but I know his reputation, and if he tells you that this will is unimpeachable, then you can take it to the bank."

"I'll believe it when I see it," Jeffrey said. "In the meantime, we've still got a big job ahead of us." He turned to my grandfather and me as he added, "Would you two excuse us? I'm hoping to get things much more settled by tonight, but that means that Renee and I are going to have to work hard to do it."

"We'll leave you to it," I said. I stood, and my grandfather joined me.

After we were out in the hall, I heard some noises coming from the dining room, and I figured that Charlotte, Tristan, and Sarah were having their own lunch. As we headed toward the staircase, I was pleased to see that the door to the dining room was closed. At least we wouldn't have to parade by them.

"Jeffrey's really coming into his own, isn't he?" Moose asked me as we headed toward my room.

"He does seem more confident than he ever did before," I said. "Then again, inheriting a few millions from your late boss could do that for you."

"Don't forget what Crane said, Victoria," Moose said. "It's more like a hundred million."

I stopped in my tracks. "How does someone amass that kind of fortune?"

"You'd be surprised. Curtis made his share of the family fortune grow, from what I've heard."

"No wonder Charlotte wasn't all that eager for him to get rid of it."

"It's enough to give her a motive for murder," Moose said.

"From the sound of it, it gives all of them motives, including Jeffrey."

"I still have a hard time seeing him as a cold-blooded killer," my grandfather said.

"It's a possibility that we have to consider," I said as we got to my room. I opened the door, and I could swear that I felt a chill on my neck as I did so. I didn't believe in ghosts or haunted houses, at least I didn't think I did, but that place really gave me the heebie-jeebies. "Just let me grab my phone and we can go," I said as I leaned down to pull the charger out of the socket.

The only problem was that my cellphone wasn't on the other end of it.

"It's gone," I said as I searched the floor around where I'd put my phone.

"Are you sure?" Moose asked me as he got down on his hands and knees and helped me look. "I can't believe that someone would just steal it like that."

"Why not? Do you honestly think that they'd draw the line at theft after they committed *murder*?"

"It doesn't make sense. My own phone doesn't work here half the time. Who are they trying to keep you from calling?"

"I wish I knew," I said. "This is aggravating."

"Let's ask Humphries," Moose suggested. "He might know something about it."

"How could he possibly know that?" I was irritated, but I knew that it wasn't Moose's fault. So, why was I taking it out on him? "I'm sorry that I snapped at you."

"Please, you'll have to do a lot better than that to offend me," my grandfather said. "Now, let's go find that butler and see if he can help."

We walked out of the room, but instead of heading downstairs, I decided to go back to the hall where that secret passageway ended. I wanted to see if I could find the release from the outside; otherwise, it didn't make any sense. After all, I doubted that someone would sneak into my room before I got there, slip into the passageway, and then wait for me to fall asleep. That thought *really* unnerved me, and if I could find some kind of release mechanism in the hallway, I'd feel much better than I did at the moment.

As I started pressing panels at random, Moose asked, "Victoria, what are you doing?"

"I'm looking for a catch," I said as I kept probing.

"A catch?"

"You know, a release, a switch. Whoever was in my room had to get in there somehow."

Moose looked relieved to learn that I hadn't lost my mind entirely, and he started helping me look. After five minutes, though, we'd both come up empty.

"This is pointless," I said as I stood up.

"We can't give up yet," Moose said. "It's bound to be here somewhere."

"What we need to do is open the door from the inside," I said. "Maybe that will give us a clue about where the release might be."

"It's worth a try," Moose said, "but we don't want anyone

to know that we found the passageway, do we? It could be our trump card before this is all over."

"You're right. I'd still like to get a better look inside, though."

"We could always check it out," Moose said. "Candlelight isn't perfect, but it's going to have to do."

"If I had my phone, I could use the app I've got that lights up like a spotlight," I said.

"You can do that?"

"I can," I said.

"Then let's go look for Humphries downstairs. That's what we were planning to do anyway when you got distracted, remember?"

"Fine. Let's go look for him."

The butler was downstairs in his office, a small space that barely looked big enough to turn around in. "Humphries, do you have a second?" I asked as I tapped on the door.

"Of course," he said as he stood automatically. "But first, I may have something that belongs to you." He reached into the top drawer of his small desk and pulled something out. "I believe this is yours."

"How did *you* get it?" I asked him as I grabbed the cellphone and opened it. It had one partial battery icon showing on the display, a charging amount that should last me a few hours before it died completely.

"One of the staff found it in the hallway," Humphries said.

"But I left it charging in my room," I protested. "Why would anyone move it?"

"Perhaps you accidently kicked it into the hallway yourself," Humphries said.

I didn't believe that was a remote possibility for one second, and I was about to say as much, when Moose grabbed my arm.

"That's probably exactly what happened," my grandfather said as he applied a little pressure.

"Thanks for finding it for me," I said as I tucked it into my pocket.

I was nearly out the door when he spoke again. "What was it that you wished to speak with me about?" he asked.

"I just wanted to thank you for setting up our private lunch today," I said. It was the first thing that I thought of, and I'd decided to go with it.

"It was my pleasure," he said automatically.

"We'll leave you to it, then," I said, and Moose and I walked out of the room.

"What was that for?" I asked him once we were back in the hall alone.

My grandfather just pressed a finger to his lips, and then he pointed toward my room.

Once we were there, I asked him again to explain himself.

"Victoria, something's going on here, that much is obvious, but the more questions we ask about certain subjects, the more suspicious people are going to be of us. It's the same principle as the missing box that was supposed to hold our discoveries from Curtis's room. Have you noticed that *no one* has pressed us about that, lately? It's kind of odd, don't you think?"

"I do, now that you mention it," I said. "Why do you think that is?"

"I'm guessing that whoever killed Curtis wants us *all* to forget about it. The longer we go without saying something, the more chance they think that they might get away with murder."

"That's wishful thinking on their part, if you ask me," I said.

"Me, too, but why give them any reason not to be complacent right now?"

"I can see that," I said. "Well, at least we can check out that secret passageway."

"Are you willing to give up the last of your precious battery charge to do it?" Moose asked with a slight grin.

"I'll sacrifice it gladly," I said as I opened the door to my room again. "Let's start exploring."

"After you," he said, and ninety seconds later I was down

on my hands and knees tapping out the odd combination on the outlet that freed the panel from its release.

Ten seconds later, I had my cellphone's torch app on, and Moose and I stepped into the secret passageway, hoping to find something, anything, that might lead us to Curtis's killer.

Chapter 22

"Who goes to the trouble and expense to build something like this?" Moose asked as we stepped into the narrow passageway together. The app on my phone allowed me to adjust the brightness of the light, so I dialed it way back. For one thing, we didn't need that much light, and for another, I wasn't at all sure how much of a charge I had left on the battery.

"When you have that much money, do you think it matters all that much anymore?" I asked. "If it hadn't been recently used against me, I would have loved a space like this once upon a time."

"Maybe," he said. "Hey, what's that over there?"

The door was closed behind us, and the darkness was pretty complete outside of my light. "I don't see anything," I said as I scanned the walls.

"Look back at the door we just came through," he said.

I shined my light back where Moose was pointing, and I saw a board the size of a loaf of bread that didn't quite match its surroundings. As I got closer to it, I saw that it was attached at a single pivot point by a shiny nail that reflected light back at me in the surrounding gloom. There was a faint scent of something in the air, as though it had been recently lubricated with something that smelled industrial to me. As I played the light over the board, I noticed that there was a bent nail holding the whole thing in place, and after I moved it slightly, the board swung down, and I could see that there was a peephole that opened directly into my room. I'd been right after all.

Someone had been spying on me.

"Let me see," Moose said, and I stepped aside so he could look for himself.

He pulled away quickly. "That's just not right, Victoria."

"How do you think I feel?" I asked. "Moose, this is getting more personal by the second. I really want to catch this killer."

"We're assuming that the peeper and the murderer are one in the same, aren't we?"

"I hate to think that there are *two* creeps running around this place," I said. "Let's keep looking." I slid the board back into place and latched it back with the bent nail.

The passage led to the hall, just as I'd found earlier.

"You're right. It's a dead end," Moose said.

"Not quite," I said as I showed him the hidden exit. "This leads to the hallway where we all congregated last night before we went to bed. Look, if you stand right here, you can see what's going on out there."

Moose did as I asked, and after a moment, he said, "The coast is clear. Should we sneak out this way and look around?"

"I'm not finished searching this passageway yet," I said. "But I *would* like to find the release switch from the inside."

"Let me try something," Moose said as he gently pushed on the center of the wall.

The door swung open silently, and I smelled something again, a fresh acidic aroma.

My grandfather looked pleased as he turned to me. "There's no reason to disguise it in here, but I'd love to know how they accessed it from the outside."

"I'm not even sure that it matters a whole lot at this point," I said as I reached out and pulled the door closed again.

"Why did you do that?" Moose asked. "I could finally see in here."

"I didn't think that it was prudent to let anyone know that we found the secret passageway," I said.

"Good thinking. Do you mind if I borrow your light on the way back?"

"Be my guest," I said as I handed it to him. Before I let it go, though, I looked at the battery. "I'm not sure how much time you've got, though. The charge is nearly gone."

"I'll be quick," Moose said. He took the cellphone and held it closer to the wall where we'd just passed by. He walked a ways, and then he turned quickly and walked back. Running his hands against the exposed plaster and lath, I could see that he was searching for something.

"What are you looking for?" I asked him.

"Give me one second," he said. "There it is," my grandfather exclaimed a moment later. "I knew that it had to be here."

"What did you find?"

Instead of replying, Moose pushed on a piece of plaster that looked segmented, and part of it slid to one side. "You're not the only one being watched from here," he said. "There's a peephole in my room, too, and if there's a way to watch, I'm guessing that there's a way to get in as well." He kept pushing different parts of the wall, and suddenly a section of it opened up.

Moose poked his head out, nodded, and then he pulled the door shut again.

"They were watching both of us?" I asked.

"I don't know if they *were*, but they *could* have been." He held a hand up, and then he took in a deep breath. "Do you smell anything?" Moose asked me.

I took a deep breath myself, but other than the mustiness of the passageway, I couldn't smell a thing out of the ordinary. "No, whatever it is, it's too subtle for me to pick up."

"Exactly," Moose said. "This door wasn't lubricated like the other two were."

"So, whoever did it meant to spy on me all along," I said.

"It appears that way," Moose said. "I'm not exactly sure why that is, though."

"Just pile it on top of all the other things we don't know," I said. "Let's keep looking for another access door."

We searched until my battery died completely. There wasn't much space left that we *hadn't* covered, so I was pretty confident that we'd found all that there was to see in this particular passageway.

"Maybe the killer didn't even know about the peephole into my room," Moose said. "That could explain why it wasn't lubricated."

"I'm not sure what good that knowledge is going to do us," I said.

"Hey, it's just a little more information than we had before, and knowledge can't be a bad thing to have."

"No, but I wish we'd get something a little more directly relevant to the case."

"All we can do is try," Moose said as he secured the secret door to my room behind him.

I grabbed my charger and plugged in my cellphone again. My grandfather noticed what I was doing, and he asked, "Aren't you afraid that the killer might steal it again?"

"No, I have a hunch that he or she is done with it. Why else make it so obvious to find?"

"I can see that," Moose said.

There was a tap at the door, and I opened it to find Humphries standing there.

"Yes?" I asked him.

He looked troubled. "I knocked earlier, but I didn't get a reply."

"We were too busy talking to answer it then," I said. How else could I explain that the reason Moose and I hadn't answered his earlier summons was because we'd been exploring a secret passageway?

"Very good," he said. "Ms. Trane would like to see you."

"I'm sure she would," Moose answered. "The question is, do we want to see her?"

"I believe so," Humphries said with a slight nod.

"Then lead on," Moose said.

"What do you think this is about?" I whispered to my grandfather.

"I don't have a clue," he said with a grin.

"That's true in more ways than one, isn't it?" I asked.

He laughed slightly. "Don't be impertinent. You're in the

same boat that I am."

"I never denied it," I answered with a grin.

It faded quickly away when I saw Charlotte Trane's expression. She looked as though she'd just swallowed something bitter, and it wasn't going to go away anytime soon.

"I've been told that I need to be more forthright with the two of you," she said. "I would like the opportunity to do that now."

"It would make for a nice change of pace," my grandfather answered.

"Let's hear what she has to say, Moose," I said.

He looked at me, and then he turned back to Charlotte. "My apologies."

"There's no need," Charlotte said. "This situation has put all of us under a great deal of stress. I know that I haven't been all that welcoming to you. I mean to correct that right now."

"That sounds good to me," I said. "Did someone say something to you?"

She looked even more uncomfortable now. "Let's just say that I've been shown the error of my ways and leave it at that. Now, how may I help you?"

It suddenly occurred to me that in our questioning, we'd never asked Charlotte directly where she'd been when Curtis had been killed. "Would you mind telling us where you were when your brother was murdered?" I asked.

I glanced over at Moose, who looked absolutely thunderstruck. He had to have just realized that he hadn't been aware of our mistake, either. At least one of us had caught it.

"I was in conference with my niece and one of our attorneys," she said. "Why do you ask?"

"I hate to pry, but what was it about? And would you give the attorney permission to speak with us about it?" I asked. "I know that you're not comfortable doing this, but it's important."

"Certainly. It was regarding her ex-husband, a flea of a man who wouldn't go away. I understand that you already know that my brother paid him off. I wanted to make sure that he didn't come back later for more, and I needed Sarah's cooperation to do that." Charlotte reached for a nearby telephone, dialed a number, and then after barely three seconds of waiting, she said, "Mr. Barlow, I'd appreciate it if you'd tell the woman I'm about to turn you over to exactly when and where we were when my brother was murdered." There was a slight pause, and then I saw Charlotte's lips tighten. "I'm sorry. Were you under the impression that was a request? Very good." She handed me the phone with a slight smile. "I had to remind him who keeps his law firm afloat."

After getting confirmation from the attorney, I handed the telephone back to her.

"Is that satisfactory?" she asked.

"More than you can imagine," I said. "You don't happen to know for sure where Tristan or Crane were, do you?"

"I haven't any idea," she said. "Is it important?"

"It might be," Moose said just as his cellphone rang. "Excuse me," he added as he stepped away from us. "I really need to take this."

As he moved away to have a whispered conversation with whoever was calling him, I said, "We appreciate your cooperation."

"I only hope that it helps."

"It already has," I said.

Moose came back, clearly agitated. "Victoria, could I speak with you for a second outside, please?"

"Of course," I said as I turned back to Charlotte. "We won't be long."

She didn't reply, so I followed Moose down the hallway and out the front door. "What's so important all of a sudden?" I asked him.

"That was Sheriff Croft on the line," he said.

"What did he want? Did he find Crane?"

"No, I asked him about it, but this doesn't concern Curtis."

"Then what was it about?"

"He found out what happened to the mayor," Moose said.

"Was it really some kind of assassination attempt?" I asked.

"It turned out to be nothing as sinister as all of that. Jack Higgins was mowing his lawn across the street and his riding mower kicked up a piece of gravel and flung it through the mayor's picture window. By the time that rock finally got to him, it wasn't traveling fast enough to do much more than nick his arm a little. The sheriff said that a Band-Aid and some antiseptic fixed him right up."

"It's nice when it *doesn't* turn out to be attempted murder, isn't it?" I asked.

"You've got that right," Moose said.

"Should we go back inside and get back to work?" I asked my grandfather. "Is there anything else that Charlotte can do to help us?"

"I don't think so. To be honest with you, that place is starting to feel like a gilded cage to me," my grandfather said, the irritation obvious in his voice. "Victoria, do you feel like taking a walk? There's supposed to be a great path around the property that runs through the woods. It might clear our heads and allow us to clarify our thoughts."

"That sounds great to me," I said. "I'm getting a little cabin fever myself."

"Then let's do it. It starts right over there."

As I started on the path, I told my grandfather, "Whoever snuck into my room to retrieve what we found had to be someone who might be implicated by the contents."

"I think you're right, but what did we have that was so valuable? Sarah already explained the check, and besides, she has an alibi. Tristan didn't get any money from his uncle even though he asked, so that could be a motive. Then there was the check written to Crane, but we don't even know where he is right now."

"We can't forget that Jeffrey had a reason to want to see what was in that box, too."

"And he even tried to get us to turn it over to him at least twice last night," I reminded him.

"Okay then, we've got it narrowed down to three suspects with different clues for each of them and no solid alibis that we can prove or disprove for any of them. We're a pair of bang-up detectives, Victoria."

"It doesn't help that we're running out of time, too," I said. "We've got until the memorial service in the morning before all of our suspects scatter in the wind. If we think it's hard now, imagine how difficult it's going to be once they're all gone."

"Let's face it," Moose said. "We're in a real bind here."

"Then maybe it's time to push them all even harder," I said. "What's the worst that can happen?"

"The murderer gets tired of messing with us and decides to eliminate us both," Moose said.

"Sure, that's one possibility," I said. "Then again, more pressure might just lead to the truth about what happened finally coming out." I tripped on something, and saw that it was a metal rod drove into the ground identifying a nearby plant. As I picked it up, I asked my grandfather, "What does this look like to you?"

"It's just a botanical stake," he said without hesitation.

"Think about it in more recent terms," I said.

"It could be a duplicate of the murder weapon, couldn't it?" he asked as he took it from me. "Right here on the grounds."

"We need to show this to the sheriff," I said.

"I'm guessing that every last one of our suspects had access to one just like it," Moose said.

"This is getting darker and darker," I said. "Moose, if you want to, we can pack up and go home right now, or we can do our best to finish what Curtis asked us to do. I for one vote that we stick it out, no matter what, but if you want to throw in the towel, I'm with you."

"I'm not going anywhere," my grandfather said. "We'll see this out to the very end, no matter what."

I was about to hug him when I noticed some movement on the path behind us.

Someone was watching us!

I pulled close to my grandfather and whispered in his ear, "Moose, somebody's behind us."

"Turn around very slowly when I release you," Moose said. "I'm going to see if I can catch whoever's back there."

I wasn't about to let my grandfather charge off into the woods without me. "We both go at the same time. Ready, set, go!" I said as I let him go and started running.

We never even got close.

By the time we broke free of the tree-lined path, whoever had been eavesdropping on us was long gone.

But how much had they heard or seen?

Chapter 23

It would have helped us a great deal with our case if we could have found one of our suspects panting and out of breath once we were back in the house, but we weren't about to be so lucky. By the time we saw them all gathered again, everyone was seated around the dining room table for the last meal of the day. Whether by design or accident, we were again following the house rules of eating together.

"Won't Renee be joining us?" Moose asked Jeffrey as the first course was about to be served.

"She had a date," Jeffrey said, more than a little glum because of the news. "She explained that she had planned it weeks ago, and she hated to stand the man up. She'll be back first thing in the morning, though."

"Surely you're not going to work on the day of Curtis's memorial," Charlotte said, the disapproval thick in her voice.

"I don't have much choice," Jeffrey said. "The official reading of the will has to occur tomorrow at noon. It was my boss's last request, and I plan on following it to the letter." There was nothing said about who the new beneficiary was, and I couldn't blame Jeffrey for trying to get one more night of peace before the Trane clan found out that they'd all been snubbed by Curtis.

"I can't imagine why Uncle Curtis insisted on that," Sarah said. "Tristan, do we really have to do it that way?"

The artist just laughed at his sister's question, and I could see his fingernails were still spattered with paint as he clutched his glass. I had a strong feeling that there was something a great deal more potent in there than the water the rest of us were drinking. "What makes you think my opinion counts for anything around here?"

"That's no way to behave, young man," Charlotte said.

"Maybe not, but I for one am truly sorry that he's gone.

Can any of the rest of you say that?"

Of course there was a chorus of protests, no one louder than Jeffrey.

"You're out of line, Tristan," he said.

"No doubt you're right," he said, though he didn't seem all that regretful to me. Tristan stood, and I could swear that he had to balance himself a little as he did to keep from falling down. "I've lost my appetite all of a sudden. Give Cassidy my apologies. I'm going to bed."

"Tris, that's no way to act," Sarah said as he tried to grab her brother's arm.

"Let him go, Sarah," Charlotte said.

He nodded, and then paused at the door as he saluted us. "Good night, all."

No one but Sarah wished him good night back.

"He's hurting inside; can't you all see that?" Sarah asked as she stood.

"It looked to me as though he was trying to kill the pain with alcohol," Jeffrey said.

"I will not tolerate that at my table," Charlotte snapped out. "I did as you asked today and told Moose and Victoria everything I could, but there are limits."

"Charlotte, you and the other Tranes, including Curtis, it pains me to say, have coddled those two for far too long."

She shot him a look that would have withered someone with less reason to be immune than Jeffrey was, stood, and went after her last living relatives.

Jeffrey frowned, and then he threw his napkin down on the table. "She's right. I've got to get this chip off my shoulder. After all, there's no reason for me to have one now. I'm sorry, you two, but I've suddenly lost my appetite as well. I'm going to have Humphries bring me a tray to my room." As he stood, a flash of lightning lit up the room, followed too closely by a crack of thunder. "It looks as though we're in for another stormy night. Make sure you know where your candles and matches are."

After he was gone, it was just Moose and me.

That's when Margo wheeled out a cart laden with food. She looked surprised to see only the two of us.

"Don't be shy," Moose said. "Nobody else might be hungry, but I'm starving."

I didn't even try to hide my smile.

"And you?" she asked me.

"I'm eating as well. There's no sense in this lovely meal going to waste."

Moose and I had the loveliest poached salmon, steamed broccoli, squash, and peas, and finished up with small lemon tarts. "They don't know what they missed," Moose said with a satisfied smile.

"I'm sure they're all eating in their rooms. I saw Margo make several trips upstairs with trays."

"Then they missed some good company," Moose said.

"No doubt," I said.

"Right now, I feel like a—" He was interrupted by his cellphone. I couldn't wait to get my own back.

"Hey, Sheriff," Moose said. "What's up?"

His grin died suddenly. "Really? You're sure? Okay, thanks for calling."

After he hung up, my grandfather looked at me and frowned. "That was odd."

"What did he have to say?"

"The authorities just stopped Crane at the airport in Nashville a few minutes ago. The man had cleaned out all of his bank accounts, and he had a one-way ticket to Belize in his bag. The sheriff says that it's just a matter of time before he cracks and confesses to the murder. They're going to start the extradition process tonight."

"Crane? Really?" I asked.

"That's what the man just said."

"It doesn't make sense," I said as I pushed my dessert plate away. "How did he get to Nashville?"

"The sheriff said that he drove," Moose said.

"I don't believe it," I said. "Logistically, it just doesn't make sense. Moose, Nashville is a good six hours from here. Whoever was spying on us was around here three hours ago."

"That's true, but are we certain that whoever followed us is really the killer? Could it have just been something more random than that?"

"Why *else* would anyone follow us, Moose? Crane might have done some bad things, but I don't think that he killed his boss. Curtis just paid him off, remember? Why would he *kill* him?"

Moose looked around. "It's a little too public here for a discussion, don't you think?" he asked as Margo walked in and started clearing dishes away. "What say we adjourn to your room?"

"I'm not staying there, not in a thunderstorm," I said. I'd walk home before I'd go through that again.

"You don't have to," he said soothingly. "I promised Greg that I'd take care of you, and I meant it."

"I promised Martha the same thing," I said with a grin of my own as we climbed the steps.

"Why don't the people we love trust us not to get into trouble?" my grandfather asked.

"Oh, I don't know, maybe because of past experience?" I asked with a smile.

My grandfather laughed, and then he held my door open for me. "Why don't we talk about it while you pack?" he asked. "Working on the assumption that the business manager didn't do it, what do we have to lose by pursuing the case on this end in the meantime? If we're wrong about Crane, all that it means is that we ruffle a few more feathers while we're here."

"I'm not worried about that," I said. "Are you game?"

"You know I am," Moose said. "So, who does that leave on our list of suspects?"

"Just Tristan and Jeffrey now, as far as I'm concerned," I said.

"Can you really see either one of them doing it, Victoria? Jeffrey doesn't seem like a killer to me, and I'm not sure that

Tristan had the guts to kill Curtis, let alone do it in front of everybody at the diner."

"I don't like either suspect myself," I said, "but we really don't have any choice."

"You might be right, but I don't have to like it. I hate to say it because I like the man, but Jeffrey is by far the strongest suspect, in my opinion."

There was another crash of lightning, and the afterimage was burned into my retinas. The explosion of thunder afterward was deafening. I waited for the lights to go out, but they flickered for a few moments, and then they came back on.

I quickly threw my things together as I said, "I like Tristan for it myself. There's something that I'm missing, but it's just barely out of reach. I'll get it. Just give me a little time."

"I know you will," Moose said. "Is your bag ready?"

"It is," I said, and we left my room and headed for his bedroom next door. I knew that technically I wasn't any safer there than I had been in my room, but I certainly *felt* better.

"Now, why don't you get settled in, and we'll figure out how to trap the real killer," Moose said. "While you're doing that, I'm going to brush my teeth."

I nodded as I unzipped my bag. That's when I realized that I'd left my cellphone and charger back in my room. "I'll be back in a flash. I forgot my phone."

"Want me to go with you?" he asked as he held his toothbrush six inches from his mouth.

"Don't be silly. I'll be fine."

"Okay, but when you get back, be prepared to be brilliant."

"I will if you will," I said with a grin.

I left my grandfather in his room and hurried next door. The cellphone was just where I'd left it, and I had a full charge, though I didn't have any signal. The storm must have been doing it. As I grabbed everything, another bolt of lightning flashed, and the rumbling was even deeper. The lights held again.

But the real killer had taken advantage of me being distracted, and was now standing between me and the doorway.

It appeared that I had just used up my last bit of luck.

Chapter 24

"What gave me away, Victoria?" Tristan asked as he pointed a gun at me. From the way he spoke, I realized that he'd never been drunk at all. He'd had to get away from that dinner table in order to ambush me back in my room. The oddly amusing part of that was that at that point, I hadn't even realized that he was the one who'd done it.

"The turpentine," I said. "I smelled it in the passageway, and then again in your studio." I knew that if I stalled long enough, Moose would barge in. Which way would he come, though? I might be able to turn Tristan toward the door or the secret entrance, but I couldn't make him face away from both of them at the same time. I had to be ready based on the slightest clue, or my grandfather would be walking straight into a trap.

"You realized that?" he asked. "How very clever of you. I don't understand, though. Surely there couldn't have been that much turpentine on my hands. How did you smell it? I've used it so long myself that I've grown inured to the odor."

"Did you use it to clean the hinges on the passageway door?" I asked. It had taken me until the moment before Tristan broke in to realize that the smell from the passageway was also the smell from his studio.

He shook his head and smiled. "I didn't even think about that connection. Very good. Surely that wasn't the only thing that gave me away though, was it? That nearly made it the perfect crime."

"What will the police find if they search your room?" I asked. "Will they discover the outfit you wore when you killed your uncle in my diner?"

He looked at me smugly. "That's all been taken care of."

"How about your shoes?" I asked, and I saw that I'd

scored a direct hit again.

"I never thought about that, either," he admitted glumly.

"It turns out that you weren't nearly as good as you thought you were," I said. "Why kill him now, Tristan? The man was dying anyway, and as far as you knew, you were going to get a quarter of his entire estate."

"You didn't know about him threatening to sign a new will? I overheard him on the phone. He was all set to give all of his money to that mongrel of his, so I had to stop him."

"What are you talking about?" I asked him, truly puzzled now.

"You didn't suspect? It turns out that I know something that you don't. Charlotte found out about Jeffrey long ago and hired him just so she could keep him under wraps working in her house in San Francisco. They were never supposed to meet, not with a continent between them, but Curtis popped in unexpectedly, and the two got together and hit it off immediately. My uncle hired him and brought him back here. Charlotte probably nearly died when that happened. No one knew about their real connection, though. Charlotte must have thought that she was safe, but I realized it from the moment I saw Jeffrey. They walked the same, and they even had the same snort when they laughed. He wasn't really an orphan after all. Everyone else figured it was just because the two of them were so close, but *I* knew the truth. I have an artist's eye for such things."

"Jeffrey is Curtis's son?" I asked, not able to take it all in.

"Keep up, Victoria. Didn't I just say as much? I had a feeling that Curtis suspected it himself a few days before I killed him. You see, I couldn't afford to wait any longer. I knew that Uncle Curtis wouldn't do anything until he had a DNA test done, but time was ticking, and if I hoped to inherit what was rightfully mine, I was going to have to move fast."

"But if Jeffrey really *is* his son, doesn't that make all of this rightfully his, not yours?" I asked.

"I am a Trane, not him!" Tristan shouted. "That's what my aunt and uncle were fighting over the night before he died. She was going to try to stop Curtis, but he told her that it was already too late. He was bluffing, though."

"No, as a matter of fact, he wasn't."

"What are you talking about?" Tristan asked me, his voice suddenly growing hoarse.

"He already signed the new will. You killed your uncle for nothing."

"You're lying!" he shouted just as another flash of lightning hit. This one took out the lights, and the roar of thunder afterward was deafening. A shot rang out, and I knew that I was out of time. I couldn't get to the door, but I could reach the switch for the secret passageway. I stabbed it as another flash of lightning blew up around us, followed by another, and another. It was as though we were in the middle of some kind of heavenly battle.

I couldn't risk standing, so I crawled toward the passageway door. If I hurried, I might just get out with my life.

I shoved it aside and hurried in, but as I did, a hand grabbed the door from above my head as I tried to close it.

I hadn't been quick enough after all.

Abandoning that plan, I headed for the exit, but as soon as I heard Tristan roar behind me, I knew that I'd never make it. The only thing that saved my life was the darkness in the passageway. I couldn't see anything, but neither could my attacker. Instead of going toward the hallway, I stopped at the entrance to Moose's room.

I hoped that he was ready for me as I shoved the door open and crawled inside.

He wasn't, though.

Apparently I'd just outsmarted myself.

The room was empty, and Tristan was right behind me.

Chapter 25

"Nice try, but you're just postponing the inevitable, Victoria," Tristan said. "You have to die. You see that, don't you?"

"Haven't you killed enough?" I asked as I searched for something to fight back with. The only thing nearby was a chair, and it easily outweighed me. I couldn't lift it over my head to hit him.

I might be able to shove it at him though, but I had a feeling that would just make him laugh.

"Any last words before I pull the trigger?" he asked me.

I looked up at him, ready to spit on him in one last defiant act, when I saw my grandfather looming behind him.

"Moose, be careful. He's got a gun."

That made Tristan laugh. "*Really*? *That's* your last play on this earth?"

"No, but it might be yours," my grandfather said as he smashed Tristan in the back of the head with a heavy brass lamp.

He went down in a tangle of arms and legs, and I knew that he wasn't getting up anytime soon.

I scrambled for the gun, and then I told my grandfather, "Call the police, would you? I'll explain it after they get here."

"There's no need. I was in the passageway all along."

Moose used the cord from the lamp and wrapped it around Tristan's arms and legs. Let him get out of that.

"I was afraid that you were going to stumble in and get shot," I said as I made it to my feet.

"I nearly did, but then I heard you two talking. I was going to sneak into your room through the passage as a joke."

"That's not even remotely funny," I said.

"I realize that now," Moose said contritely. "When I

figured out what was going on, I was about to burst in and help you when I heard the release click. There wasn't room to do anything in the passageway, so I went out through the door in my room, circled around, and then ended up following you both back into my room through the passageway again. Forgive me?"

"Well, you *did* just save my life, so I suppose we're even," I said as he hugged me.

Moose pulled out his phone, and then he frowned at it. "I can't get a signal."

"Let me try the landline," I said. "Sometimes they work in the worst storms."

Finally, a little luck came our way.

I got a dial tone, and soon after, Sheriff Croft promised to be on his way.

Chapter 26

"I don't understand," Jeffrey said as the police hauled Tristan away. "What do you mean?"

"Curtis was your real father," Moose said as he put an arm around the man's shoulders. "I'm sorry that you found out this way, but we just learned of it ourselves."

"He was always so good to me," Jeffrey said, "but this?"

"To be fair, I don't think that he knew himself until the end," I said. "Charlotte, on the other hand…"

"She *knew*?" he asked me, his voice filled with anger.

"That's what Tristan said," I told him.

At that moment, Charlotte and Sarah came in together. "What's the meaning of this?" the elder woman asked.

"Get out," Jeffrey said, the anger seething in his voice.

"What? Have you lost your mind?" Charlotte asked, but I could see a hint of fear in her eyes as well.

"I just found out. How could you have kept us apart? What kind of monster *does* that to someone? I understand that you never cared about me, but he was your *brother*!"

"Watch your tone, Jeffrey."

Jeffrey looked at her for a full ten seconds, and then he started to laugh, low and soft at first, but finally bursting out loud. "You can't talk to me that way."

"We're family, whether you like it or not."

Sarah looked at her aunt, clearly confused by the recent developments. "Aunt Charlotte? What are you talking about?"

"Hush; we'll discuss it later," she said.

"I meant what I said. I'm the executor of this estate, and the only beneficiary. I want you both out of here, and I mean right now. If I have to call the police back here, I'll do it, and gladly. I'm sure the newspapers wouldn't mind a tip, either."

"You wouldn't," Charlotte said. Did she shiver a little as

she said it? "It's pouring out there."

"Then I suggest you take an umbrella with you."

I was about to say something when Moose touched my shoulder lightly. I glanced over at him, and he shook his head briefly. He was right. No matter what was happening here, this wasn't any of our business.

"Go. This is your last warning," Jeffrey said.

"Come along, Sarah," Charlotte said as she wrapped an arm around her niece.

"I don't understand *any* of this," she complained, but she left with her aunt nonetheless.

After they were gone, Jeffrey said, "I'm sorry that you had to see that." He looked into my eyes and added, "You probably think that I was a little harsh just then. Think of it this way. What if you didn't know that Moose was your grandfather, and someone kept it from you your entire life? How would you react?"

I didn't need long to consider it. "I would have probably been tougher than you just were," I said as I squeezed my grandfather's hand.

"Good. I hope we can still be friends after this is all over."

"Absolutely," Moose said, "but if it's all the same to you, I think we'll head back home. Don't worry, we'll be back for the memorial, but I've completely lost my taste for the Pickle Palace."

"Come on," Jeffrey said as a sudden smile blossomed on his face. "I'll drive you."

"You don't have to do that," I said quickly. "We can call my husband."

"I insist," Jeffrey said. "Besides, I *want* to do it. It's a nice way to honor my late father, don't you think?"

"I think it's perfect," I said.

As Jeffrey drove us home through the storm, I glanced back at the Pickle Palace as the lightning lit up the sky one last time. It looked as though the storm was about to break, and I could see clouds parting to show us the stars.

It was a shame indeed that Jeffrey had missed out on having a father, but knowing how close the two men had become over the last three years, there was some solace to be found there.

For me, my family was everything to me, and I knew that I was blessed with grandparents and parents that loved me, as well as a husband I adored.

I knew that I'd never have as much money as Jeffrey had, but where it counted in the riches of those who loved me, I was the wealthiest woman on earth.

MOOSE'S PEACH COBBLER

We love to make peach cobbler at my house, especially in July when the peaches are in season. In a pinch, you can use canned peaches if you have a craving for this dessert in winter, but nothing beats fresh! The delightful aromas coming from the kitchen while this dessert is baking are enough to make it worthwhile in and of itself, but when you've had your first taste, wow! Some folks like vanilla bean ice cream over this, but I like it plain, warm from the oven, along with a tall glass of cold milk.
Enjoy!

Ingredients
Peach Mixture Filling
fresh peaches, 3 cups (about 3 large peaches) peeled, pitted, and sliced
lemon juice, 1-2 teaspoons freshly squeezed (enough to coat the peaches)

white sugar, 2 tablespoons
dark brown sugar, 2 tablespoons
cornstarch, 1 teaspoon
cinnamon, 1/4 teaspoon
nutmeg, 1/4 teaspoon

Cobbler Topping
All purpose unbleached white flour, 1/2 cup
white sugar, 2 tablespoons
dark brown sugar, 2 tablespoons
corn starch, 1/2 teaspoon
baking powder, 1/2 teaspoon
salted butter, chilled, 4 tablespoons
hot water, 2 tablespoons

Directions

Preheat the oven to 425 degrees F. Peel the peaches, pit them, and then cut them into thin slices. Add the lemon juice and stir thoroughly. In a separate bowl, add the sugar, brown sugar, cornstarch, cinnamon, and nutmeg. Mix thoroughly, then add to the peaches, mixing thoroughly again to coat the peach slices. In a small pan, spray with cooking spray, then add the peach mixture. I like using small loaf pans and splitting this into two portions. Bake for 8 to 9 minutes. While the peaches are baking, in a separate bowl, add flour, white sugar, brown sugar, corn starch, and baking powder, and mix thoroughly. Then add the chilled butter, incorporating with a pastry blender or a fork until little balls are formed in the mix. Next, add 2 tablespoons very hot water, stirring just enough to make a paste.
Take out the peaches at their allotted time and add the topping, spreading the mixture out onto the peaches. Don't worry about covering the top completely, it's not necessary. Bake for 25 to 35 minutes, or until golden brown on the top, remove from the oven, let it cool if you can wait that long, and enjoy!

This recipe makes enough to serve 4 people, or 2 very hungry ones!

MOM'S SOUTHERN SWEET TEA

This must seem too easy to need a recipe of its own, but a great deal of the outcome of making good sweet tea is in the process, and we've honed this one to perfection over the years. The secret is that proper sweet tea must be sweetened while the tea is still warm. A warning first, though. It may be too sweet for your taste, but if you want to see what real southern iced tea tastes like, you could do a whole lot worse than trying this recipe. Not for the faint of heart!

Ingredients

water, boiling, 1 quart
water, cold, 1 cup
white sugar, 1 cup (adjust to taste)
tea bags, 5 (we like Lipton, but some folks we know swear by Luzianne. They use 6 tea bags instead of 5.)

Directions

Put the tea bags in a pitcher (1 1/2 to 2 quart size), something sturdy enough to handle boiling water! Glass or thick stoneware is best; plastic can melt, and aluminum can add its own strange taste. Bring a quart of water to a gentle boil, and then pour the water over the teabags. Make sure that they are soaked in the process, and steep them for about an hour. Around half an hour into the steeping process, add 1 cup of sugar and stir it in thoroughly. Taste it, and then add more if you need to at this point. After an hour or so of steeping, remove the tea bags and discard, then add about 1 cup of cold water and stir it in thoroughly. Let the tea cool completely, since ice will dilute it enough so that you'll notice it if you try to rush it. After it is cool, drink up and enjoy!

Makes 1 quart sweet iced tea.